D0908658

An Instinctive Feeling of Innocence

THE SWISS LIST

Dana Grigorcea

An Instinctive Feeling of Innocence

TRANSLATED BY ALTA L. PRICE

LONDON NEW YORK CALCUTTA

swiss arts council
prohelvetia

This publication has been
supported by a grant from
ProHelvetia, Swiss Arts Council

This publication has been
supported by a grant from
the Goethe-Institut India

Seagull Books, 2019

ISBN 978 0 8574 2 651 2

British Library Cataloguing-in-Publication Data
A catalogue record for this book is available from the British Library

Typeset by Seagull Books, Calcutta, India
Printed and bound by WordsWorth India, New Delhi

An Instinctive Feeling of Innocence

1

A metallic shimmer brought on by the impending storm flattens the city's depth, turning it into a painted backdrop like the ones at the Diamandi photo studio, where my glamorous grandmother had a scandalous portrait taken as Bucharest's first woman in a short skirt. She's shown on the arm of my grandfather who, complete with walking stick and gangster hat, impatiently steps out into the haze of time.

Now, in the approaching weather, Bucharest looks like a nostalgic backdrop before which no pose would appear out of place—quite the contrary, I'd say.

I sit on the marble steps of the National Savings and Investment Bank and smoke my absolute last cigarette before quitting for good—very consciously ignoring the fact that the pack will have two cigarettes left which will compel me to exert the discipline indispensable to my profession and duly complete whatever I've started. But I'm not granted the peace and quiet for a last cigarette.

'I beg your pardon, Madame Director, but with your permission, we should leave now, before the storm breaks. Your colleagues are leaving too.'

Our chief security officer calls almost all his coworkers 'Director' or 'Madame Director'. This does not annoy those who actually are directors and who—according to our Director of Team-Building and Adherence to European Standards—should only be differentiated from all other employees by the fact that they're allowed to eat fish with their hands on company outings.

We just call our chief security officer 'Chief'. After all, we're striving for a level playing field.

Was I the one who gave the security people permission to go? The police files leave that open.

I stand outside, before the large sliding door, my back to the coworkers heading out for the evening. I breathe the smoke in deep and blow it out again, watch the blue cloud float a few feet off the ground and, through it, see the Museum of National History across the street. One step back would set off the smoke alarm.

Twigs and leaves flying by appear to divide the distance to the shopping arcade below into smaller and smaller segments. Flavian is waiting for me there. Last week he was appointed head of the Romanian Institute of City Planning—quite a coup. 'Since no one else wanted the position,' he'd told me on the phone. Be that as it may, we want to celebrate.

5

The curved skylights' yellow light fills the Macca-Villacrosse arcade with a murky, viscous air, slowing down the passersby. Through a few broken window-panes I spot an Egyptian shopkeeper restocking yogurt, and just hope the air won't smell too much like wet dog amid the hustle and bustle.

Under no circumstance do I want to spend hours cooped up in Flavian's SUV talking about the old farts at his institute, our eyes fixed on the flashing-red rain-drops, one of Bucharest's classic traffic jams as a back-drop. Dinu, my previous boyfriend, had procured a blue police light for such occasions; as soon as he set it on the roof, the chaotic traffic parted, although not as neatly as it might have, so he had to honk the horn, too, and yell out the window, 'What if it really were an emergency, you assholes?'

Now that I'm on leave after the incident, I'm reading a book about Bucharest in the 1800s that quotes a British naval captain, Charles Colville Frankland, who, on his way back from Constantinople, found Bucharest full of golden carriages bearing boyars clad in crimson robes and fur. A French general raved about the city's many coaches and new-fangled carriages with liveried coach-men, although he criticized the slow traffic, as 'there were still some old Transylvanian carts, in which rode Noah's whole clan, pulled by eight, ten or even twenty horses whose foals trotted round freely'. The manure was brought to the city's outskirts, piling up into mounds. Once dry, they were set on fire.

I wonder if I should smoke the cigarette down to the filter, the last extravagance of my historic addiction.

Lightning flashes like a strobe. Blindingly white seagulls dart past the magnificent neoclassical buildings lining Victory Road and down towards the Dambovita River. Someone who's probably been shouting this entire time now yells out a woman's name even louder, Stanca or Bianca. I wonder whether Flavian is already there, and has had to wait for me.

I stub out my cigarette and try to go back into the bank. The door is shut tight. I peek through the windows—has everyone already left and locked me out? It seems so. Regardless, I knock on the windowpane, savouring the humiliation my all-consuming addiction has brought on, because that's what will shield me—the young, oh-so-successful bank clerk—from a relapse. The side door that only security officers are allowed to use opens, and a young guard lets me in so I can get my purse.

I have no convincing explanation for why that took me a full twenty-five minutes. The policeman ventures a guess that it didn't register because a new guy at work left earlier than my professional conscience would allow me to, and so I'd had to linger a bit in the draughty Macca-Villacrosse arcade. I leave it at that.

At the police precinct, my uniform is wrinkled and the make-up that usually gives me the look of a cheerful stewardess is all smudged. It's no wonder the officers aren't misled by my first name, Victoria, which often leads people to think I'm part of the post-communist generation and therefore presume I'm ten years younger.

My tiff with the young security guard is harmless.

'Where's the animal-rights group's donation box?'

'Back there, in the storeroom,' he says without turning.

'It's supposed to be in the entrance hall.'

'The boss moved it.'

'But it wasn't there during the day, either.'

He turns, slightly amused, and suddenly it was clear I'd just lost a touch of respect.

'It was in the storeroom.'

'In the storeroom?'

I grin back at him. He reminds me of someone, and it's not an unpleasant reminder. If I took a step towards him, we'd fall on top of each other.

'But it has to stay in the entrance hall, otherwise nobody can give a donation,' I reply.

He turns back around. 'The boss said someone could steal it from there.'

The echo of our voices breaks free for a moment under the high glass dome. I roll the animal-rights group's donation box back into the entrance hall, as the security guard repeats 'We're not supposed to do that' a couple of times. It's clear he's trying to convey that my action can be undone without him having to lay a finger on me or the donation box. He jams his fists into his pants pockets, and when that doesn't work he sticks his foot out in front of the donation-box wheels but then draws it back. 'Just do that tomorrow, when the boss is here.'

'The boss, or the Director?' my voice thunders up into the glass dome.

We laugh. And that's when we first notice the old man beside us.

The man tosses one of those cheap, reusable nylon bags between us. 'Ladies and gentlemen, this is a bank robbery!'

He looks like he stepped straight out of a film noir, wearing a hat and long trench coat, with a revolver bulging in his left pocket. He really looks a lot like an actor who recently died—his name escapes me but he was a legend—a B-movie actor, actually, whose burial sparked a nationwide debate about how to reconcile cremation with Romania's orthodox Christian traditions, if that were even possible.

'What now?'

'The money!'

'What money?'

The security guard and I look at each other. This guy is senile. As I should've made clear later on, at the precinct, I always try to force myself to be sympathetic to old people, even if it's just because of their white hair, but I don't always succeed—because I know that these old folks aren't really old folks, at least not the way their forebears were. These new old folks only wear the cheap mask of old age, and behind it they're still just the children of communism, their shifty eyes darting about. They are as young as their malevolence is all-encompassing .

I remain polite as with all clients, regardless of their requests, and explain why we can't just hand him the cash, how the foreign-exchange transactions work and why the conversion process prevents us from doing so. The old man sighs—or was that the security guard, whose respect I've certainly just regained?—and then says, 'Damn speculators.' I maintain my professional smile, somewhat softened by closing time, and tell him that's above my pay grade, and no one currently present is authorized to provide any further information on the matter.

As the old man points his revolver at the security guard, I cut the performance short and fill the sack with bundles of banknotes. Without another word the man turns and exits the bank through the sliding door. Why the security guard follows him I can't say—anyway, he takes the animal-rights donation box with him.

I hear gunshots ringing out from the street.

2

During halftime I go to get some elderberry juice, and Flavian follows me out onto the balcony. Spotting the wicker bottle I fill with dried elderberries and lots of yeast to brew my special seasonal drink, he stands there agape. His gaze prompts me to bake some blackcurrant biscuits to go with the juice.

'I still have some dough in the fridge,' I lie, insisting that he stay in the living room to watch replays on TV. I do so in the presumption that he'll also furtively flip through the channels and see some of the news spots which by now must be showing the bank robbery and a bunch of mothers in mourning—a peasant woman in a black headscarf amid other women in black headscarves, all keening at the top of their lungs.

As I come back in with the botched biscuits, FC Rapid Bucuresti scores a goal. Shouts of 'Gooooooal!' rise from the streets, and Flavian might even have hugged me had the winner not made such a spectacle. The multiple replays show a levitating Daniel Pancu intercepting the ball with his heel as he descends, kicking it from afar into the corner of the net.

'You get to see more goals at home,' says Flavian, scarfing down my burnt biscuits.

'Gooooooal, goalgoalgoalgoooooal,' shout the commentators, the south stand catches fire, 'Gooooooo-ooooal,' shout a bunch of neighbours, even on the replays, and my eyes tear up, as they always do on such occasions.

As my grandma Mémé's second husband lay on his deathbed—he was a gaunt man, scarred by his time in a hard labour camp on the Danube Canal—he hoisted himself up one last time and shouted out, with a croaky voice and half-chewed communion wafer in his mouth, 'Go Rapid!' His confessor, a strict priest from the Stavropoleos Monastery, responded 'Amen, amen, amen.' At his funeral the brass band even played the FC-Rapid anthem—a beautiful melody, fit for any and every occasion, that's why it goes, 'We're at home all over, every goal, every gate opens for us.'

'And now you have to stay put,' Flavian tells me, 'because it seems you're their good-luck charm.'

Rapid wins four to two. 'What a night,' the TV host says, before the night has even begun. It's the night Flavian is supposed to move in with me, as he doesn't want to leave me alone following the bank incident.

I lead him into the master bedroom, and we lie on my parents' bed—the only bed in the house, since I turned my childhood bedroom into an office when I moved back home. It's a high bed with a built-in spring mattress with two deep indents where my parents used to sleep, quite far apart, I point out. We lie down in the dips and repose like two expired souls sculpted atop a stone sarcophagus. Our hands folded together on top of the sheets, we stare up at the orderly procession of lights reflected on the ceiling from the passing cars.

'Want another glass of water?' Flavian asks.

'No thanks.'

For the past two days I've been constantly chugging water, since everyone, everywhere had offered me a glass and, given the circumstances, drinking every glass had struck me as the only appropriate response.

'You?' I ask Flavian, to break the silence.

'Not right now.'

'Maybe we should keep a bottle next to the bed, so we don't have to get up in the middle of the night.'

He laboriously gets up, sets a carafe of water and two glasses on his nightstand. 'Nice glasses.'

'They were my grandma's.'

He circles the bed, sets a glass on my nightstand, takes my head between his hands and looks into my eyes.

'Just wake me if you're thirsty, OK?'

He kisses me on both cheeks and my forehead, circles back round the bed and, wearing the long-sleeved black silk pyjamas he'd folded up as small as a handkerchief to fit his briefcase, slips back into the sheets that smell of lye. Mrs Jeny swears by tradition, and has once again washed the linens with her homemade detergent. It took a lot, but I finally convinced her not to clean the furniture with kerosene. I wonder why I'm now getting a slight whiff of it.

'Do you mind if I open the window?' Flavian is already asleep.

With the windows open, the city's silence seeps into the room even more than when they're closed.

The silence then swells into an ever-louder sound of crickets, and their chirping comes in waves, almost dissolving all peace and quiet, transforming it into a muffled restlessness.

Now, thanks to the ongoing investigation and the state of shock I'm supposedly in, I'm on leave for the first time since moving back from Zurich. And because I'm on leave, I can no longer shirk the administrative duties that come with the houses, woodlands and vineyards returned to my family, not to mention the family's four plots at Bellu cemetery. The crypt's northern wall is usually lined with the stubs of burnt-out candles. The caretakers tell me someone comes there at night to perform a complicated ritual cursing an enemy—it must be a very old someone, because this has been going on since I was a child. 'Poor great-granduncle Neagu,' my mother complains, but she's actually lamenting the decayed statue of women in mourning, leaning against the crypt wall, clothed only by their long hair. 'It's by Raffaelo Romanelli! You simply must find the vandal, we owe it to our ancestors.' Hiring the security firm that covers my bank is clearly no longer an option.

Heat and the smell of linden blossoms fill the room, and the heat intensifies the sweet scent. My throat is scratchy, and I can tell I'm going hoarse even though I'm not saying a word. Three or four times I hear engine noises, their ups and downs remind me of a hilly landscape. Machines menacingly race up towards me, then fall back into the waves' valleys.

In the morning I call my parents in Nice again. They have guests and are tipsy. 'C'est notre fille, qui est rétourné à Bucharest,' I hear my father say.

'Ah, oh,' the guests reply.

'C'est romantique!' my mother says, and they all laugh approvingly, 'C'est romantique!'

I laughed along, but just cannot get used to how loud they are now. During the long summer nights of my childhood, when we had friends over and sat under the grape arbour beside the house, they always spoke softly, almost silently, so that even someone on the second floor would think we were completely silent, or no one was there. Had there been a spy, he'd have had a heart attack when one of us tapped the wine cask to replenish our spritzer. Back then the nights were so dark that I couldn't tell whether I was still under the arbour or somewhere else, whether my eyes were open or closed, whether I was actually moving or just thinking of moving. At the time I enjoyed that kind of confusion, a staggering feeling of weightlessness—indeed, when I think back, I recall a primal blamelessness, an almost instinctive feeling of innocence.

The scent of linden continues its spread through the nighttime air, following me to bed, where we lie motionless—two warm bodies, unable to cool down in this heat. The sky remains bright and starless. Through the window, on a nearby hill, looms the brightly lit People's House, surrounded by seagulls floating slowly up and down on the air as if in a snow globe. 5,100 rooms, 200 toilets, 480 chandeliers, 150,000 incandescent bulbs—I count it all and fall asleep.

The bright ceiling light suddenly pierces my eyelids. I'm lying in bed, the windows are closed, the room has cooled down a bit. Flavian is hopping around half-naked, the top of his black silk pyjamas in hand, hunting mosquitoes.

'Don't worry,' he says, 'with a little damp toilet paper we'll easily wipe all the blood spots off the walls.'

I sit up on the edge of the bed, and as my eyes regain their focus the last mosquito falls to the floor, leaving a red speck under a portrait of my great-grandmother. She's shown in traditional garb and leather shoes, in front of a painted backdrop of a pastoral landscape and haystack. As Flavian delightedly admires my great-grandmother and congratulates me on her good looks as if complimenting a baby, I wonder who the mosquitoes might have bitten.

All sorts of noble relatives look at me with a smile from their baroque picture frames—Mémé's uncle Neagu poses with a hand on the lapel of his short fur coat, and can't seem to stifle a fit of laughter. Turning the frame over reveals a right-slanting note in light blue ink which must be tickling him from the reverse side of the picture, 'Neagu, perennially good-humoured, portrayed here in a splendid Romanian shearling jacket.'

There's a bang, and the light goes off—either the bulb's burnt out or a fuse is blown. The last traces of light float in my vision as if someone had taken a photograph of me with the flash on. Flavian says something, standing not even an arm's length away. I grab the silly silk pyjama top from his hand and toss it into the darkness.

Judging by the scorching heat, when we finally get up it's already late morning. A beam of light slants into the room, and sparkles of dust dance in the air. The contours of the rococo furniture decorated with golden garlands gradually take shape, as does the painting by Nicolae Tonitza, *Girl with a Red Cap*, and the photos of Mémé's venerable relatives, all of whom I know only from these images. As I get up, I see the painting of

Danae and the shower of gold reflected in the Venetian mirror and, as usual, feel as if someone were standing right behind me—the only thing missing is a startling voice yelling 'Your ticket, please!'

There's a taxi parked in front of the house, waiting for my neighbour, Madame Pharmacist. Flavian and I, still nude, lean onto the windowsill to look out through the linden leaves and past the flower-patterned quilt my neighbour Codrin airs out over his windowsill every day, just as his grandmother did when he was still a bed-wetter.

When I head to the bank each morning, the pharmacist's taxi is already out front, the driver just hanging out with the door open, reading the newspaper or a book, settling in for a nice long break. At some point, he folds the newspaper, sits up at the steering wheel and honks. After a while Madame Pharmacist—Aristita—sprints out to the pavement, her long grey hair streaming, and blithely gestures, 'Start the engine!' That's how it is every time.

A burly street-sweeper in a yellow jumpsuit with a smiley face on the back sweeps his way past the yellow taxi, whistling the melody of the song that goes 'Heaven, I'm in heaven, and my heart beats so that I can hardly speak . . .'. Flavian thinks it's by Glenn Miller.

'Hey Smiley, who's that song by?' Flavian calls after him.

The gypsy looks up into the lindens, and, when he can't make us out, flips his middle finger in our general direction.

And then, as usual, just as the driver has almost given up on her, Aristita runs out, her long grey hair streaming, and the taxi engine revs up like an aeroplane. Its noise fades into the distance as they drive along the Dambovita River towards the People's House, and soon Smiley is also out of sight, his melody almost out of earshot.

Still framed by the window, we hug, and Flavian's breath tickles my neck. I talk and talk, telling him about my neighbours who—all of a sudden, as if to spur on my storytelling—come out of their apartments and amble across the street. I haven't seen most of them for years and now here they are again, at once so familiar and so foreign, much like the ancestors gazing out at me from the photos and paintings all over the house. Their stories come easily, and with every story I tell him, Flavian and I grow closer.

3

We immediately recognized him as someone of high rank, judging by his movements and mien. It was clear as soon as he and his confused-looking wife moved into the very flat where the crime had taken place, shortly after the gruesome events. They strode dead ahead, hand in hand, both wearing prim hats and carrying little suitcases, as if returning from a spa resort. Just the previous day the building superintendent had replaced the nameplate, whose perfectly chromed surface now read 'Mr N. O. Iosif, General of the Reserve'.

My family stopped hosting regular afternoon films but still had their friends over, and the house had the same conspiratorial atmosphere—green curtains drawn tight, greenish sunlight glinting off their coffee cups. 'Want a filtered cigarette, Maria?' 'Sure!' 'Despina, dear, bring that pack Sorin gave us!' 'Sssssshhh, no need to scream, Dimi!' 'Sorry, darling.' We sat on the Persian carpets Mémé had brought back from her travels, rife with holes marking paths trodden in another flat, in another life. My parents and their friends from university sat cross-legged in front of the massive armchairs, and the silence surrounding the rococo furniture of my unknown yet illustrious ancestors slowed down all gestures, giving everyone a solemn feeling of déjà-vu.

Maybe that's why I remember all the details of the murder on the first floor, because the brutal facts no one could forget brought me closer to the memories of that period—of my childhood—and it was the first time I could share them.

I tell Flavian about how our neighbour Nenea Sandu spent hours tinkering with his car several times a week after work. He'd set the radio on the railing, the timeless classics of Angela Similea and Mirabela Dauer wailing from its speakers on weekdays, the nasal voices of sports commentators on weekends. He usually lay halfway under the car, wearing sweatpants, or shorts when it was hot out, his bare torso smeared with oil. He and my father always recited the same dialogue, giving our good neighbourliness a sweet sense of reliability.

'Greetings, Nene' Sandu! All's well?'

'Just fine, thank you. I'm down here, working on the car.'

'How's Auntie Felicia?'

'Busy with her own stuff.'

'And little Codrin?'

'The rascal's out playing.'

Each evening he'd take the water hose from the garden and wash the car, carefully soaping it up with a sponge, rinsing off the suds and drying it with chamois. Then he'd pull up the weeds growing between the street's cobblestones, water the roses in front of the house and the vines in the side yard, pull a tarp over the car and go upstairs to join Auntie Felicia. Late each evening, ever the hard-working man, he'd take out the garbage, whereupon Auntie Felicia would call out, 'Sandu, dear, no one takes the garbage out in the evening, it brings bad luck,' followed by his dismissive yet reassuring grumble, 'Whatever.'

When Mémé visited, she paid no attention to Nenea Sandu as he worked out front. She considered him a low-class, pot-bellied communist parvenu who'd set up camp in her late father's house.

Our neighbours' laughter echoed into our bathroom every evening through the vents. I patiently waited as they bathed their son, sitting with my hair already shampooed, until they were done and the warm water would return to our side of the plumbing. Sometimes my mother would heat some water on the stove so I wouldn't have to wait so long.

Each summer the family car was ceremoniously brought out. Nenea Sandu and Auntie Felicia carefully folded the protective cover and stowed it in the trunk, strapped their large suitcases and cooler to the roof rack and opened the windows of the fully packed car. 'The Iancus are taking off, come watch,' my father yelled out, and we leant over the windowsill, peering down through the lindens' rustling branches.

The Iancus came back at the beginning of autumn with deep tans, perennial stories of barely survived mishaps and spontaneous roadside picnics and a bag full of stolen sunflower seeds as booty.

Who would ever have thought that these people, who seemed so steady in their eternal routines, would meet their downfall in a crime of passion?

'Did you see it coming, Dimi?' my mother asked.

My father replied that he hadn't.

The disaster began its unforeseeable course when Nenea Sandu evidently took a lover, something no one could've imagined, and this lover was none other than Aristita, the pharmacist on the ground floor, the only neighbour Mémé could stand conversing with.

Aristita was single and flirtatious and, as previously mentioned, took a taxi from home to work and back every single day. I think it irritated Nenea Sandu, especially when the taxi parked too close to his precious car. At some point, however, he befriended the taxi drivers, and started chatting with them about this and that until Aristita arrived. Then he watched the taxi for a while as it drove off, idly stood below the linden tree and listened to the radio. Back then one of Mirabela Dauer's hits was played increasingly often, 'The water-wheel turns, whoosh-whoosh-whoosh, the heartbeat burns, whoosh-whoosh-whoosh . . .'.

Soon Nenea Sandu worked less and less on his car. Sometimes he'd only pull the tarp back as far as the driver's door, get into the front seat and just sit there for a while in the dark.

One warm autumn day he decided to spend three days with his lover, or so the story now goes. So he carefully packed a small suitcase—or had his wife pack it for him—said he was going on a business trip, and moved into Aristita's shady ground-floor flat.

It was a calm autumn evening, a bit hazy, the asphalt shone in the heat. Hundreds of crickets chirped, first nearby, then in the distance, then up close again. We were at the window, waving to friends who were just leaving the house, and heard them greet someone downstairs. It was none other than Nenea Sandu who'd just brought out his mistress' garbage. 'Greetings, Nene' Sandu! All's well?' our friends called out. My father, too, said hello from the window.

He had returned to his own flat that evening out of habit, sleepwalking straight from the dumpster to the first floor, wearing his blue-checkered robe and slippers. When he found the door locked, he rang the bell once, twice, several times. Finally, when his bewildered wife opened the door, he strolled in with the wrong garbage can and went right past her, yawning.

What followed was soon in the paper, and gruesome details flew throughout the neighbourhood. We were told that an indiscreet policeman had confided the story to friends but we had been in the room directly above, and, despite the building's paper-thin walls, we heard only the trees rustling outside, the pigeons cooing under the roof. Not until dawn approached did we finally hear a scream, then sirens, and see lights flashing through the mist. Looking down into the closed-off courtyard, we saw the garbage can amid a handful of policemen. Nenea Sandu's legs stuck straight up above the rim, a slipper stuck on one foot.

Auntie Felicia was taken away, and little Codrin stayed behind, effectively orphaned. His grandparents soon moved in to take care of him. I remember how one of my parents' friends, Rapineau, commented, 'This is one for the history books,' hinting at how the ever-clever General Iosif had managed to get rid of his step-son in order to make room for himself to move into the distinguished neighbourhood.

In the greenish afternoon light, coffee and hot chocolate were served, the last spoonfuls of sugar were shared and the film our friends had brought was pushed into the rattling VCR. During the film, which almost everyone knew by heart from previous gatherings, the conversation came back to the murder. Where had the hatchet come from, why didn't we hear a thing, and how had this petite woman managed to drag her stout husband down the stairs and then shove him into the garbage can?

Being neighbours with the General was annoying but we kept to ourselves and always greeted him. I can still picture how he slipped a bit on the handrail of the stairs each Sunday, dressed in white from head to toe, a tennis racket under his arm. Mémé always returned his friendly hello.

Codrin went on to become a model student, his uniform always perfectly starched. I remember bringing our share of the cleaning lady's fee for maintaining the stairwell to the General's wife, and even from the hallway before I entered I saw the framed photo of a student in blue uniform. 'That's our Sandu—oh, what am I saying? I mean—that's Codrin, of course!' the General's wife said, inviting me in. She was quite petite, had perfect posture, and her white, perfectly coiffed bun made her seem just a bit taller than she actually was. But I refused to be misled by her grandmotherly facade, as I was sure she wanted to ensnare me, to lay some sort of trap so she could later denounce us as the class enemies we really were. She kept me at the table, set with perfectly polished silver flatware, and served rabbit stew with olives.

'Do you like rabbit?' she asked.

'I like everything,' I said.

She leant over the table and said, conspiratorially, 'Me too. But sometimes I feel sorry for them.'

I still associate her with this memory, after all these years. She showed me around the flat and was very nice, and I thought maybe she was just an addled old lady, and one might come to the conclusion that it was I using her. I always kept an eye on the door, to see whether the General had returned unannounced from tennis or hunting, accompanied by some important comrade. I remember the flat was quite bright, and full of mirrors. In the bedroom hung two portraits, one on each side of the bed: a black-and-white, slightly blurry picture of the General's wife as a young girl—it could easily have been Mémé at a ball—and a hand-coloured picture of the old general in civvies, just like I always saw him, but with slightly blushing or maybe even rouged cheeks.

4

Instead of heading right, towards the opera house, where I usually take the trolley or a taxi to the bank, I turn left and my legs immediately go numb. Strolling through my nearly forgotten old neighbourhood, I only realize that I've been wearing the high heels I usually wear to work as I turn off Dr Joseph Lister Street onto Dr Carol Davila Street. The light-speckled asphalt, scented and sticky from the fallen linden blossoms covering the ground, comes into glaring sun as I pass the tennis courts. Blinded by the light, I turn away and for the first time see the vast view over the high walls lining the courts; as children we'd try to scale them, and their rough, antique plaster finish made us all the more determined to clamber to the top.

We'd swing ourselves up onto the wall's tiled roof, and use pruning shears to cut bunches of white and purple lilacs until Bebe, the fat security guard, came to chase us away with a water hose. We'd dance across the wet tiles, taunting him, 'Doofus, doofus, you can't catch us,' and then leap off, our arms full of lilacs. Bebe waddled after us, purely out of duty, but only for a few paces. By the third fence pole he reached the tree stump in front of the therapist's house, where he'd plop down with a noise that never failed to provoke Ms Miclescu's dogs. They'd bark at the metal fence until a window opened on the first floor, and the therapist's mother leant out, water bottle in hand.

'Steer clear!' Ms Miclescu shouted from her office, and her old mother actually managed to hit not only the excited dogs but also the sweaty Bebe as she flung water at them from above.

Neighbours could do nothing to comfort Bebe after the many reproaches he endured over the years spent guarding the local headquarters of the party with the three-rose logo and ever-changing names, a gathering place for the old nomenklatura, the nouveau-riches and others of their dubious ilk. The fact that the party had moved into this particular neighbourhood, instead of settling into some anonymous grey building in the midst of its electorate, struck everyone as an affront. They plastered the area with political posters, and sent out invitations to Charleston-themed dance parties and Brigitte Bardot–themed film soirées, all in vain. Supposedly not one neighbour had ever set foot in the place—in fact, most crossed the street when walking by, so as not to fall suspect.

Mémé had told me that this situation was her fault. After Romania became a socialist republic, she purportedly drew a dear friend's attention to the vacant building. The government had expropriated it and, later on, none of the former owners had come forward to claim it. Mémé's friend was a grandmaster, and was looking to open a chess centre for children but she didn't follow through. Instead, she gave the tip to an acquaintance who, together with three friends, sought a headquarters for his newly founded minority party. It had a large basement and well-shaded garden for their bacchanals. But then their minority party went bankrupt, and in the end there was just one party member left, who'd sit in the courtyard listening to Demis Roussos records at full volume on his gramophone, 'Come into the garden of a thousand melodies . . .'. Ultimately the minority party of the soon-forgotten name was incorporated into the ominous majority party of the ever-changing names, and with it went the local headquarters in our neighbourhood.

The lilac has now grown tall and is once again in bloom, harbinger of a mild autumn. Thanks to my high heels, I catch a glimpse into the courtyard I'd never set foot in, and discover my neighbour Codrin. Although I haven't seen him since moving back to town, I've arranged to have him pay the rent via deposit slip, just like all the other tenants.

'Ave Caesar,' I call over the wall. As a kid I called Codrin Caesar, although I've forgotten why, and it always annoyed him, for reasons I've also forgotten. Back then, we'd sometimes run into each other in the backyard, and spend an hour or so hanging upside-down, our legs bent over the railing where our mothers beat the carpets clean, until our parents called us in.

Codrin looks up from three cannibalized bicycles, probably gleaning parts from one to fix the others. Above his head I spot the party logo with the three red roses, and colourful posters on the left and right, whose large letters proclaim 'Wheels for Kids'.

'Don't worry. I didn't see a thing, and I'm going now, anyway.'

'Hey, Victoria—no, stay. It's not what you think!'

He comes to the iron gate, and we greet each other with a peck on the cheek. He smells fresh and citrusy, like cologne, and has rolled up his white shirt-sleeves. 'Finally our paths cross, finally,' he intersperses, 'since when have you been back?' I reply, 'Oh, for a little while.' He turns red in the face and talks about this and that, about his job in an uncle's law firm. Then he asks me about the bank in Zurich, and I sense that I'd better start speaking in bank lingo so that my high heels don't look like they're just a disguise.

'Want something to drink?' he asks.

'You promoting the party bar now, too?' Codrin blushes again, and I remember that he used to turn red a lot—it was the model student's only visible emotion.

After all, this was the guy about whom everybody had started saying, 'If only he were a bit different, he'd be all right,' which meant that his unhappy environment prevented him from being who he really was, so to speak. I disliked him by the time we were teenagers for that same reason—because he was so vague, it was so hard to pinpoint the real Codrin, that everyone was obliged to be nice, just in case.

And so I greet him like an old friend but also leave rather brusquely. He notices, and at the last moment asks how I'm really doing. I can tell he has read the papers and knows about the incident at the bank. I admit I'm on leave now, and have to take on more family chores as well.

'What are you munching on, without offering any to your friends?'

'A homeopathic cure for headaches,' I say, and he nods.

'So, you believe in homeopathy . . .'

'Can you lend me a bicycle?'

He looks at me, slightly stunned.

'What, do I have to be a member?'

I hand him my high-heels and step into the pedals. The front wheel wobbles with every turn but stabilizes as I gain speed.

'Do you know how to ride?' he calls after me.

'Better than your commie asshole friends.'

As soon as I'm on the bike, its devilish wheels start to turn all by themselves, as if the road plunged steeply downhill. As my speed increases, so does the summer heat, and so do the insects—bugs or bits of dust hit my face and arms, and with every fence I pass more dogs bark, the sound swells over the street, towards the houses, into the courtyards and backyards, and over the echoing stairways and balconies. In the staccato rhythm I've built up, the neighbourhood is opening up to me, in all its twists and turns: not a soul as far as the eye can see, just as it's always been in the Cotroceni district, as if life were one endless Sunday afternoon. Only the new car models stand as witnesses of the present, proving the unpredictability of technological advancement. Before, most cars were covered with dusty plastic tarps, their wheels sunk into the asphalt, weeds growing below their rusted bodies. Back then, the automobile seemed an outdated means of transportation.

I lift my legs, stretch them out like wings, tap one of the gates with the tip of my toes and bump into a car parked diagonally on the pavement with the tip of my other toes. A car alarm goes off, and one after the other the dogs resume their howling.

At the corner of Dr Petre Herescu Street, the pavement becomes uneven where the powerful roots of a mulberry tree burst through it, and the bike's front wheel loses its way. I love the knotted root patterns in the asphalt, and although I probably don't know all the houses in this area—above the first floor, most of them disappear into the trees—I know every pavement by heart, by the texture of its tree roots. I could always go for walks at night without stumbling, and during the day I always just looked up. As the neighbourhood ballet teacher was fond of saying, 'A *lady* always looks straight at the tree tops.'

Across the street there used to be a cute barbershop filled with mirrors. My father was a regular, and every time he'd ask the owner, 'Do you know my daughter?' And every time the barber would answer, 'How could I not?' The shop is gone now—the building was demolished, and now there's just a deep hole filled with water, requiring round-the-clock pumping. The place used to shine so bright, its many mirrors opening and closing in dazzling panels. One summer I found that same shine again, at the Kafischnaps cafe in Zurich, on a bright Sunday morning.

The deafening din of the water pump prevents me from hearing Dinu, who greets me from the roadside and sees my joyful surprise—a delight I hadn't foreseen granting him the many times I rehearsed this first reunion in my mind. It's as if the old mulberry tree were a cardboard backdrop he just burst through with an expert leap, his arms stretched wide behind, and suddenly I have a close-up of his large nose. I once told him that his nose reminded me of Iznogoud, the character in Jean Tabary's comics, who was always saying 'I want to be Caliph instead of the Caliph.' 'I *am* Iznogoud,' Dinu had answered, 'but a calm Iznogoud—ambition is too proletarian for me.' After we broke up eight years ago he'd travelled the world, taking ski trips, surfing trips, going on a pilgrimage to Asia.

'Now, finally, I'm a stuntman.'

As if to prove it to me, he climbs onto the bike and tells me to sit on the back-wheel rack, my knees leaning against his back. He holds the bike steady, steering it counter to the direction I'm leaning, almost falling, so we head towards Hero Square. I get off as we cross the bridge over the Dambovita, and he pops some wheelies on the bike, laughing.

As the bus from Queen Elisabeth Boulevard stops at the traffic lights in the middle of the bridge and the packed-in passengers turn to watch us, Dinu rides up the bridge's balustrade, inches a bit forward as if the bike could prance and, with my theatrical 'Nooooooooo!' as accompaniment, gently drops over the edge.

As expected, everyone onboard—driver included—got out at the bus stop around the corner and came running to the railing. A wheel could be seen sinking in the murky water but not trace of the young man. Years earlier—long ago, before the riverbed was lined with concrete—I'd seen a dead horse down there.

The streetlights turn on, and the powerful headlights of cars driving by light up a yellow sign with a smiley face that reads, 'You are leaving the Cotroceni district.' I slip off amid the chaotic traffic.

5

The old bank robber has struck again, in my own neighbourhood this time, at the Austrian bank just across from the opera, and the payoff was big. I do a rough calculation, and figure it totalled nearly a hundred bundles of 500-lei notes, portraying our national poet Mihai Eminescu and a blossoming linden branch. And because there was an ad for villas in the trendy neighbourhood of north Bucharest—that used to be the dense Baneasa Forest—just below the news article, I can't help but go on to calculate how many villas that money could buy. Dinu would've considered this a case of *déformation professionelle*—'*un*professional *de*training'—because he felt my work in the bank had warped my mind.

I can just picture the lucky robber and his long strides as he crosses the intersection that's usually deserted by evening, a heavy sack over his shoulder, past the little brick building that used to be a public toilet.

It was later renovated to become the Rio Bar, but now stands empty, and is so covered in theatre and concert posters that it looks like a gift-wrapped present. The cocky robber trips as he hoofs it across the nearby lawn, runs into the old transvestite just as she's buckling her sandal and her cracking voice startles him as she turns in reproach, 'You graceless bitch!' The bank robber and I now have a mutual acquaintance.

Then he disappears into the thick mangrove forest and soon reaches the old Doherty tennis courts—little fish and frogs swim in the stagnant water. Wading through the darkness in water up to his knees, the sack still over his shoulder, with only the stars to orient himself, he heads towards the mighty ruins of buildings that were supposed to become a communist museum. Their bulk astonished even Mémé—every day as we rode bus 368 when she took me to school, she'd exclaim, 'Good lord, how quickly they're building, it's utter madness.' Sometimes I wouldn't even turn to look, adopting the same defiant indifference with which the locals of Zurich and Paris refuse to admire the Lake of Zurich and the Eiffel tower. And then she wouldn't look, either.

In the yellowish light of the street lamps, the abandoned libraries and bakeries became reminiscent of a sleepy provincial town, unless one looked up to see the endless blocks of flats stretching up towards the pale moon. Followed not even by his own shadow, the robber ran up the street, boarded the bus, climbed to its upper level and rode it to Palace Square.

A tourist group—Serbians of Romanian descent, waving Romanian flags in front of the equestrian statue of Carl I—only notices the old man when the printer cartridge full of red ink powder explodes from his sack, and he runs off in a red cloud, like a red devil. Millions of moths flit about in the bright light surrounding the statue, and some turn red. Below them, the Serbian tourists gather around the mound of worthless paper.

'All for nothing,' says Sweetie, disappointed.

I sit quietly on the little stool by the newspaper saleswoman, and read the pages she tosses into my lap, checking what's already been read to me. The ongoing saga of the bank robber makes me happy, maybe because I'm relieved that a story whose very beginning I was there to witness is still unfolding, so I'll have some entertainment during my unexpected leave. But it's not all relaxation, since I'm now busy thinking about how I can escape this dear woman I've so unexpectedly run into again after all these years.

Sweetie, as locals called her, had been a sought-after seamstress who worked in a tiny, glass-enclosed platform cabin by the fence of our family friend, Rapineau. 'I'm going to Sweetie' was a way to show off back in the day, because it implied you had expensive silk stockings that you'd ruined by going about so carefree.

At the kiosk cafe nearby, a grumpy employee empties a water bucket onto the pavement at ever shorter intervals. Although the suds quickly evaporate on the hot asphalt, passersby still have to jump over the remaining puddles. Bossa Nova songs blare from Sweetie's little radio, chestnut trees rustle in the park, and it's almost as if the pretzel vendor of my childhood could reappear at any moment, dragging his heavy bag of baked goods across the pavement. The noise of the street swells into a monotonous wave, washing over me in my little refuge between the kiosks hawking newspapers and coffee.

I know this street so well! As a child, I took bus 368 from here to school. I probably haven't been back since then, but now I miss the street vendors with their trinkets displayed on large loops of wire. I wonder why I've begun visiting my old haunts—is it because I've fallen in love, or because I've unexpectedly been put on leave? Whatever the reason, I have to admit and accept that the floodgates of my orderly reality might well come crashing down. I got a hint of this possibility a few Sundays ago, when I spotted a little gypsy boy at St Eleutherius Church. He was wearing an ironed, eighties' school uniform, and had scraped the communist emblem off the belt buckle. Now I see him dressed in rags, running between cars lined up at the traffic light, panhandling. There's a flabby cat with striped red fur over his shoulder. It's either dead or just a toy.

'Would you like another coffee? You look a bit pale.'

So I drink the third coffee the kind woman brings me from the kiosk cafe, and I'm a bit surprised to see her tip yet another shot of brandy into her own cup, openly, as if it were simple syrup.

When my expensive tights needed darning, I'd ball them up and wrap them in newspaper, venture over to Sweetie's and knock on her window. I did this countless times as a child, and she always left me waiting—sometimes as long as it took her to finish mending an entire stocking—before glancing down from her high pedestal, eyeing me from above the rim of her lowered glasses and saying 'You've come for nothing, there's no room, I'm booked full.' After a long plea, she'd take my newspaper bundle, peek in, and with a *tsk-tsk* reply, 'Hmm, look at that . . . well, come back in a week, then we'll see.'

Gulls fly overhead in neat rows, as if pulled by invisible strings. They plummet from the gable atop the municipal hospital, swoop just a few metres above the Dambovita River, cavort through the air over Heroes' Park and fly on towards St Eleutherius Church, where they perch on one of its three crosses. The shade of the trees opens up at the other end of Heroes' Square, giving an unobstructed view of the glass-enclosed kiosks selling coffee, newspapers and flowers. There's quite a crowd, as it doesn't look like it will rain, and the streets are filled with slow-moving vehicles. All in all, it seems like a peaceful morning, if one ignores the increasing noise.

Any attentive observer would notice the florists, whose movements seem particularly sluggish in these surroundings—they look like they're in slow motion as they arrange their bouquets. On closer inspection, there's something sinister about their gestures.

After she's tossed the last newspaper onto my lap, Sweetie looks at me, and her glasses have the same sparkle as always.

'Now, tell me something good, something that'll make me happy.'

I say nothing, I simply nod—do I actually nod?—and she says 'bravo' and goes on about 'young women nowadays' whose precious youth fades away because they spend it toiling in the dreary offices of dubious multinationals before they even get a chance to experience any joy in life, a real man, a real dance, a real anything. The young women rushing by don nasty expressions, as if to confirm what's being said about them, and now I know I can't get away. If I left in a hurry it would be tantamount to confessing that I've failed in life—Sweetie would *tsk-tsk* as my silhouette melted into distance under the afternoon sun, and feel sorry for my poor parents, 'Such good people, the poor dears, what on earth did they do to deserve this . . . ?'

I used to bring her flowers—lilacs, jasmine and roses from the neighbouring gardens. Sweetie's place was full of flowers, and on some evenings, when she turned on her yellowish lamp, the cabin glowed like a precious Tiffany lamp, the colourful flowers packed in tight, a backdrop for her wine-red coif. Come to think of it, her coif has survived all the ups and downs of recent history, maintaining the same shape and colour. Now, on the head of a wrinkly old woman amid all those grey newspapers, it almost looks like a warning light, signalling people to steer clear.

The crowd in front of the kiosk is swallowed up at irregular intervals by dusty buses, and an old gypsy tries to console a student who's clearly late for class, 'Hey, honey, let me make you a bouquet, with flowers as pretty as you!'

So I stay quietly seated on the little stool and let myself be coddled by the now-elderly Sweetie who's quoting aphorisms from some esoteric book. Time passes, and more and more people hurry past the newspaper kiosk, frantically waving, maybe at buses or taxis, or maybe something has upset them, they raise their arms and curse, or just lift their arms out of prudence, disgusted, so as to avoid touching each other in the crush. As soon as a car opens its door, loud music or a nasal radio announcer's voice pours out into the street. One radio voice laughs sarcastically, 'ha ha,' then there's a click and a dial tone drowns out all the other noise on the street—the offended caller has hung up.

I see the gypsy boy crouch down, the lazy cat on his lap. He counts his money, shaking his head, and tosses a few coins into the steaming puddle before him.

'What's your name?' I'd asked the same little boy on that Sunday a few weeks ago.

'Luca,' he'd replied.

'No way is your name Luca!'

He'd laughed.

'OK, my name's Arnold.'

'That's more like it, Arnold suits you.'

I'd given him money for candles, and as he kissed my hand—he didn't even have to bend—I became aware that the candle kiosk's price list was still in the old currency, and I'd always paid in the new. I remember regretting this discovery not because I'd been mistaken, which would've been an inglorious admission for anyone in my profession, but, rather, because from now on I'd have to fight a feeling of false humility every time I went to buy candles with the usual amount.

As the sunlight grows brighter, the streets become more and more bleached of colour. Skinny dogs cross the street at a leisurely pace, it's a miracle they aren't run over. One of them is all wet, ducks into the crowd, and crosses the street several times with all the pedestrians, always obeying the traffic lights.

Suddenly he stops in the middle of the pedestrian crossing and looks around, unsure whom to follow—the people heading towards the university hospital, or those heading towards Heroes' Square. So he simply stops, plops down, looks to both sides and starts scratching his ear with a hind leg.

Drivers start aggressively hitting their horn, jolting him from his contemplative reverie. He quickly darts left, then right—where even more, even louder horns chase him. Tires squeal, and from far away I try not to lose the little wet furball from sight, perhaps compelled by some unconscious conviction that his life depends on my attention.

'He'll make it,' Sweetie reassures me. 'This is his home turf.'

I have a tendency to want to control everything. Dinu once accused me of that, saying that instead of learning to adapt thanks to proper professional training, I'd twisted everything I learnt into the aforementioned 'unprofessional detraining' that makes me rather ill-suited for daily life here.

Sweetie takes my hands into hers, for the first time since we've known each other, and I suddenly realize that the familiarity one tries to create with members of this city's previous generations is merely a self-defensive deception lonely people indulge in. At the same time, I dare not let this conclusion contaminate my other dealings with Sweetie, as there's still a possibility that I've won a smidgeon of her respect which I had to chase after as a child.

'Let's chat a bit longer, but then I'll have to go.'

The way I spread my attention around to take everything in—a quality greatly appreciated in the workplace—irritates the older people I come across, maybe to them it looks like absent-mindedness or, worse, disinterest.

Sweetie won't let go, and launches into her questions about the bank robbery. She's one of those who fear the end of the story or, worse, a cover-up.

'Did you recognize the old man?'

'He looked like someone familiar . . .'

'Who?'

I shrug.

'You're in shock,' she guesses, and keeps staring at me. 'Is Dinu being supportive?'

She seems to unconsciously be inspiring me to wax positive about my ex-boyfriend. She'd always known Mrs Miclescu had raised him well, even when he was just a kid climbing trees and scaring gypsies with a sudden 'Boooooh!' She laughs, and I go along with her laughter, although I find the whole thing unpleasant. Fortunately she gets right back to her main topic, the bank robbery.

'Have you considered contacting the other woman?'

'I have, maybe . . .'

'It's best you meet right away. I could come with you . . .'

'But you're busy.'

'Come now, how can you say that when you've grown up under my very eyes, you're like a child to me . . . It'll do you both good. People who've experienced the same traumas simply must get together.'

She rummages through the stack of books to her right, and I'm almost certain she's going to pull out a book by Coelho, because she quotes him, 'You mustn't shut down, you have to travel the paths that open up for you . . .'

Over her shoulder I spot the little wet furball again, standing by the curb next to the gypsy with the flowers. His tongue is hanging out, he's completely out of breath. And although he's just escaped death by the skin of his teeth, I see a big black dog now mounting him.

6

A historian whose name unfortunately escapes me but whose figure I can still see before me—big bags under small eyes, a long, narrow nose with wide nostrils, the worn-down look of a man ready to put all his cards on the table—had recently written that society doesn't grant people recognition for what they've done but for what is said about what they've done, or at least what they've supposedly done, 'Thus people only gain recognition when they've learnt to live with their own caricature.'

The post-revolutionary generation, including yours truly, has perpetuated this line of thinking—or so said Madame Miclescu during one of our comfy therapy sessions which are basically an hour of chit-chat. Her take was that if through this phenomenon and interaction one manages to admit all presumptions, then the effect of this very phenomenon and interaction can be considerably prolonged, such that all subsequent undertakings seem secondary, or like a private game—all the more noble as it is unnecessary.

Flavian says he'll think it over.

'Buck up,' he'd called out from behind the steering wheel of a shiny Aston Martin DB 5, 'this time James Bond doesn't have his ejector seat.'

The door opened with the same click I had expected, so this was still the predictable world we were used to. I immediately took a romcom-worthy, reflexive leap off the leather upholstery which was scorching hot under the noonday sun, my hands instinctively pushing down where my miniskirt had slid up. Flavian raised his classic Ray-Ban Cats sunglasses, smiled, and laughed without laughing, playing the part of the irresistible lover, sole witness of the previous scene with me.

Linden-scented air rushed through the open windows and the streets seemed to waver in the heat, flickering between spots of sun and leaf-patterned shadows. One wild dove calls another, cooing two short notes, and the old Securitate Colonel Dobrescu walks up, a copy of *Light*—the orthodox patriarchate's weekly—folded under his arm, and effuses, 'All that is good and beautiful pleases God.' Then he grows smaller and smaller, eventually going up in a glimmer of light as we drive through the shady streets of my neighbourhood, all named after famous doctors: Dr Joseph Lister, Dr Carol Davila, Dr Victor Babes, Dr Louis Pasteur, venerable bacteriologists, and—as if to goad my childish imagination—pioneering tropical-disease researchers. During the communist era, this gesture of naming streets after such venerable nineteenth-century polymaths struck me as a wise act of subversion, and the fact that I was allowed to grow up amid the green thickets of the Cotroceni district could only be the prelude to a divine mission—I was destined for greatness.

On Dr Jean-Clunet Street, a fat, black cat appears out of thin air, bounding towards us from the garden fence on the right side of the road. Flavian just barely spares his life, slamming the brakes, the Aston Martin grazing a jasmine bush and potentially getting scratched.

'Do you want to stop?'

'The cat seems fine.'

Flavian casually backs up, putting his arm around my seat's backrest, and I give a start as if a bus ticket-checker had tapped my shoulder.

At this point I begin telling him about my first lover, Kelemen, who was Hungarian, or his mother was Hungarian, I think, and they lived in this house on the right, where there's now a restaurant called Museum. Built in the so-called eclectic style, it looks the same as it did back then. Flavian laughs and lets a rickety old Dacia pass us. Kelemen and I always went up into the attic which had a gorgeous view of the old church of St Eleutherius; the chapel's right-hand entrance had a fresco depicting purgatory, with red devils bent over naked women, and boarding-school students had scratched every single devil—probably with a shard picked up as they filed by the wall rising from crumbly clay ground—and the naked women looked disgusted, the fear in their eyes giving way to wonder, as if they had inadvertently slid down a slippery slope towards a ring of fire and would now just let themselves drift. As we entered the room, Kelemen would call to his cat, who was never there, and then we'd both go to the window to see if she was in the garden or the schoolyard across the way. Then Kelemen would take me from behind while I looked out over the city, at the old church of St Eleutherius, with either boarding-school students or young restorers lined up at its entrance.

In the rearview mirror I can see across the city square all the way to the Statue of the Aviator.

'Up until the fall of communism, a statue of the first Communist prime minister, Petru Groza, stood there. He was a doctor, too, but a doctor of law,' Flavian says, launching into a joke I remember from childhood.

A man goes to the doctor's office.

'What's the matter?'

'This treatment regime doesn't agree with me,' the man replies.

'Who prescribed it?'

'Dr Petru Groza.'

At the push of a button, the car's minibar opens, and Flavian stops by Derby, a restaurant on Heroes' Boulevard, to get two glasses. Back in the car, he pours a few drops of whiskey to the ground from the window, and I don't ask whether they're for the soul of Prime Minister Armand Calinescu, who was executed there in 1939, or for the executioners of the Iron Guard, who were also executed there. My parents argued about politics almost every afternoon; they had inherited their differing opinions from their deceased parents, or at least they later attributed their differences to their parents. Their staunch new passion for debating the policies of the interwar period, after half a decade of communism, betrayed their pretend extravagance, their desire to connect to a life that, to hear it from them, would admittedly have been just fine. The whiskey tastes smoky, or perhaps the smoke is coming from the dense mangrove forest behind the opera, where the old Doherty tennis courts and former Venus soccer stadium used to be, where the former Hippodrome used to be—all of it former, before our time. 'Good lord, how quickly they're building, it's utter madness,' Mémé always said as we passed this spot on bus 368. 'Mon Dieu,' I'd sometimes reply, because I knew it would cheer her up. Her zany uncle Neagu was always saying *mon dieu*, although I no longer recall what kind of silly situation prompted it.

Neagu was an actor and playboy, and the main anecdote I recall about him is how he was once on tour in Paris; after an opulent night out at Le Moulin de la Galette, he was strolling down a dark street in Montmartre when, without the slightest hesitation, he let one rip. A sleepless *citoyen* leant over a balcony above and shouted, 'À votre santé, monsieur!' To which Uncle Neagu called back, 'À la vôtre! À la vôtre!' And whenever I took bus 368 down Heroes' Boulevard and caught a glimpse of the brand-new gingerbread-style blocks of flats glittering like mother-of-pearl in the night, I kept an eye out for anyone still out on their balcony who might surprise passersby with a quick 'À votre santé!' from above—but no one was up there, and there was no one on the streets, either.

At some point people started saying these residential blocks were just facades built for show, but then after the fall of communism balconies here and there were closed off with insulated glass which proved that someone actually did live there. Perhaps they used the back doors, or tunnels, since no one ever saw anyone going in or out. Flavian claims there are bunkers and tunnels below the visible city, some dating back to the Middle Ages.

The afternoon sun warms my neck as I bend over the gearshift towards Flavian's fly. The car quietly hums through a bizarrely pothole-free Bucharest, it almost feels like we're flying, and Flavian starts to ramble. I understand only a fraction of what he's saying—something about Napoleon III, who modernized Paris by creating broad boulevards to replace the old twisting lanes where barricades were swiftly built for every revolution. Soon Paris became one big construction site, whole armies of architects and bricklayers were mobilized, and new churches, halls, the opera and the Hôtel-Dieu hospital sprang up, as a feverish bout of building consumed the entire population. Eminent domain was considered a social necessity, and everyone dreamt of being pushed out—landlords of run-down residential buildings, proprietors of bankrupt factories, and everyone else thought this would be a real deal, because every building earmarked for expropriation tripled in value. The selection committees turned out to be generous, and paid without negotiating, thereby paving the way for massive speculation. At first the demolition seemed to be justified by sanitary and strategic needs, but it soon grew more arbitrary and high-handed, dictated only by the few, for their own benefit. Thanks to their social position and connections, these privileged citizens were informed about the city administration's plans in advance. As soon as they heard which neighbourhood would be torn down, they swooped in to buy up cheap properties lining the newly planned, yet-to-be-built roads; once this expropriation was complete, they reaped considerable profits, running zero risk, and of course the administration's informants got their share. Anyone familiar with Paris' architectural history—beyond what little is covered by travel guides—knows that the city suffered irreparable damage during Haussmann's reign, and nowadays everyone knows that the Tuileries Palace was burnt down during the Paris Commune.

'Relax, slow down,' I tell Flavian, and hear his hoarse laugh. 'We could still get caught speeding.'

We drive down cobblestone streets, then back onto smooth asphalt, and quickly reach Palace Square. Then a clattering sound returns, as if the car had sprouted a second engine; we're back on cobblestones and heavily potholed pavement. Flavian apologizes, then swears and strokes my hair.

'Do you want to drive?' he asks as we reach Victory Square.

I take a sip of whiskey, and gaze up at the gorgeous sky—a postcard-worthy, slightly faded sky of the sort you only find in Bucharest, greenish towards the edges.

'You crazy? You know I love being driven.'

Soon we reach Aviators' Boulevard, formerly Jianu Road, formerly Buzdugan Road, formerly Antonescu Road, formerly King Mihai Road, formerly Stalin Street. Back when Mémé was little, this portion of it was still known simply as 'On the Road'.

'I've always wanted to hit the road with you,' says Flavian. The lindens here are huge, and we pass through sunlight filtered by their leaves.

7

The sun sinks low behind Mogosoaia Palace, its surroundings immersed in the day's last bit of pink light. Sweet scents of seaweed and hay swirl through the air amid white gravel footpaths, freshly mown lawns, spiral columns, ornate facades decorated with plant patterns and rosebush-lined staircases. In such a princely setting the waning sun highlights a haystack, the last, omnipresent, shabby memorial to rustic 'Romanian-ness'. The country's cosmopolitan nobility has always returned to this concept, bearing the guilty conscience of the prodigal son—speaking of which, there's an icon in the palace church depicting his return, with a warning sign, 'Be considerate: lipstick damages icons!'

The palace, built around 1700 by Wallachian Prince Brancoveanu, came into the possession of Princess Martha Bibesco in 1920. It was the humble gift of her prince, the sleek aviator George Valentin, who had himself received the humble gift of syphilis from one of his affairs. Martha, who later claimed her relationship with Valentin had always been open, also had passionate affairs with Spanish King Alfonso XIII and German Crown Prince Frederick III, and is said to have left her ailing husband for the even nobler French Prince Charles-Louis de Beauvau-Craon, whose nobility could be traced back to at least 1500. To the surprise of her high-society girlfriends, including Mémé's big sister Smaranda, she ultimately settled down at Mogosoaia Palace and stood by Valentin, whom she described in her forty-six-volume diary as a self-centred yet lovable, flamboyant man. She supposedly restored Mogosoaia Palace using the proceeds of a novel she'd published in Paris under the pseudonym of Lucile Decaux, in which she called Romania the *pays des saules*—the 'land of weeping willows'. The phrase strikes me as a bit far-fetched, since Romania is definitely a land of old linden, oak, walnut and mulberry trees, and maybe even fir trees, but you really have to dig deep to find a weeping willow, unless you live in a lakeside palace and take it to be the centre of the whole world.

Flavian drives the Aston Martin up to the palace's main entrance, and in a rush of enthusiasm I open the door myself, before the liveried, white-gloved valet has time to reach us. 'My dear madame,' he says, taking the car keys, 'you must have patience.'

'Please don't let him lecture me,' I say to Flavian.

The valet shakes his head.

'Let it go,' Flavian interjects, 'he's just doing his job.'

'He's doing it poorly.'

'Too bad about the car,' the valet says as he drives away.

Flavian pulls me in and French kisses me. Then he whispers something in my ear—at first I only feel his warm breath but the second time he repeats it I hear, 'If you keep nagging him, he'll key the car.'

I take a deep breath, smell hay, and wonder how happy I should be—after all, I'm not allergic to pollen, nor do I suffer from hay fever the way most of my generation does.

On the stairs we cross paths with three identical-looking women, in fluttering, rhinestone-studded gowns. They beam at Flavian, who turns to me and then points out that the first was blonde, the second brunette and the third a redhead, as if they had stepped out of a story in *The Thousand and One Nights*.

'Go on,' I say, 'don't get tripped up.'

Flavian puts his arm around my waist and pulls me tightly in. All at once, we're overcome by the heat, attendees' cloying perfumes, and the smell of countless heavy dishes, reeking of meat and garlic.

The wedding is in full swing, and a colourful crowd fills the grand hall, swaying to the beat of brisk folk-tunes played by the gypsy band, with titles like 'Fine Man, Mature Tree', 'Let's do the Circle Dance',

'The Gorgeous Girl Next Door' and the quintessential Romanian classic 'Hai Iu Iu'. The waiters weave through the bouncing crowd holding heavy dishes above everyone's heads. Each platter is decked out in sparklers and tinsel, and the scent of expensive, musky perfumes mixes in with the all-pervading stench of garlic, a hallmark of this high society that adheres so closely to dear old tradition.

The official wedding ceremony has already taken place, at the small chapel in Cana, Galilee, not far from Nazareth, where Jesus performed his first miracle by turning water into wine. A film from the Holy Land is projected on the entrance-hall walls, showing a sombre wedding crowd, the women barely distinguishable from the men except for the occasional piously veiled head. In the middle, next to a young woman I presume must be the bride, I recognize former prime minister Constantin Banu, a liberal. He holds a picture showing the garden of Gethsemane—the same image all pilgrims certified by the Romanian-Orthodox patriarchy get.

The guests transformed on their way here, growing more colourful, much shriller, and the women now wear fluffy feather boas and stiletto heels. The bride, too, appears transformed. She's grown: her hair, her bosom and her buttocks have all grown, she's wearing a fringed white dress, and I realize she looks—now that the scales have suddenly fallen from my eyes—a whole lot like Princess Martha Bibesco. The bridal gown is exactly like the fringed gown in a picture hanging in the cloakroom, showing Martha beside Charles de Gaulle, his fat moustache pressed to her delicately gloved hand as he bows, inviting her to dance the Charleston during a Christmas ball at Paris' St Cyr Military School in 1926. Mémé once told me the whole story. Flavian says he feels like he's known Mémé for ages.

'Mémé,' I'd always call out when I was little, my plastic yellow bib spattered with soup, 'tell me about before, when you were little, pleeease.'

Mémé almost certainly laughed before launching into her tales, narrated as always in her trademark roundabout way.

'What else is there to tell? You've already heard it all.'

'Luckily,' I replied to her in later years, 'you tell me everything, because my parents don't tell me a thing.'

And again she'd laugh her boisterous laugh, which I so fondly recall, saying 'What can they tell anybody? Those poor dears have nothing to tell you.'

Before or after kissing Martha's hand, the otherwise reserved de Gaulle said something that caused quite a storm in the family, as it carried the whiff of a scandalous backstory, 'Madame Bibesco, vous êtes plus ravissante que Josephine!' He was referring to Josephine Baker, 'the black Venus', who had recently stolen the show at the Folies Bergère wearing a banana skirt and singing the song that made her famous, her hallmark,

'J'ai deux amours'. Martha Bibesco supposedly laughed out loud—a laugh that ensured that everyone present grew curious enough to inquire after the cause. The 1.95-metre-tall Charles de Gaulle had made a massive fool of himself, allowing the Wallachian princess to lead the dance. She jumped up and down around him, jerking his arms and legs around as her husband, Prince George Valentin, stood on the sidelines, practicing dignified restraint, chit-chatting with some grandfatherly old man—perhaps French Marshal Philippe Pétain?—about aeroplanes.

'You must be right at home here,' says a woman posing as mother of the bride, tossing me a compliment, but she looks even younger than the bride, more natural, and almost completely without make-up. I tell her she looks familiar, she laughs and says I probably just recognize her from trash TV shows. I join her in laughter and say I don't watch any trash.

Her cheerfulness is unwavering, and she tells me she was a mistress of Gabor, the famous businessman—I must know him—who owned the butcher shop that, after the fall of communism, bought a bunch of starving horses from the Buftea film studios. Since I can't remember the famous businessman, I ask about the horses, and whether they were the same ones a recently deceased actor used to ride. I can't remember the actor's name, either but he was a legend, and always played historical figures: Decebalus, last King of Dacia; Michael the Brave, Voivode of Wallachia; and others. The mother of the bride shrugs, she must have been too young to remember him.

Not far from us a high pile of dishes comes crashing to the floor. The tower had been precariously balanced at a striking angle above the guests' heads for quite some time, and as it fell with a roar the closest guests—mostly women—scattered, screaming. The crowd, however, was unstoppable, and wouldn't cease its celebration—it continued dancing wildly.

Out of the corner of my eye I look for the awkward waitress, quietly waiting until she starts to resemble the graceful Dorina, a woman Mémé—and practically all the other guests at Cumpatul, a resort near Sinaia—considered a sight for sore eyes. We all take our seats at the round tables, squeezed in tight yet sitting straight, our elbows pressed against our chests, all eyes more or less conspicuously staring at Dorina, who swoops in and out through the kitchen's swinging door balancing plates piled high, her brisk yet adroit moves lending the occasion a solemnity not conveyed by the dreadful dishes being served.

I proudly sit at Mémé's side, with perfect posture, holding my own under the heavy fur coat, slowly taking small bites from my plate. The less I take with each bite, the nobler I seem, and soon I'm only nibbling two peas a time, as Dorina bursts into the hall, trampling, then stumbling. At some point she comes to a standstill and starts to scream, or first tosses the tower of plates to the floor and then starts to scream, whereupon everyone's chairs squeak on the marble floor and the shouting, wide-eyed guests run out, followed by Dorina, rushing from the hall into the TV lounge. I'm the only one left seated in the great hall, my childish imagination granting me a regal air, and finish my feast of peas in princess-like, precious bites.

I absentmindedly ask about Gabor's health, and the mother of the bride laughs, saying it's been throughly covered in the media, whereupon Flavian steps in to protect me—having lived in Vienna for some time, and then even longer in Zurich, I wasn't up to date. 'One night, Gabor . . .' says the mother of the bride, enunciating each syllable of his name, 'Gabor jumped or was pushed into his empty backyard pool.' She chuckles, because he was still wearing his father's old wristwatch which he took off every time he washed his hands. How could he possibly have been going for a swim with that watch still on?

Flavian has already struck up a conversation with the bridegroom, a former classmate who had gotten rich in Silicon Valley. He looks exactly how I'd imagine a Romanian IT engineer in Silicon Valley to look—a bit like a short Indian, and he probably speaks English with an Indian accent. The bride is still at university, her mother tells me with demonstrative pride, studying management and business administration, at two universities simultaneously—in Bucharest and Cambridge. She even got a scholarship, although she didn't need one.

This seems to embarrass the bride—it's anyone's guess why.

She's thrilled to finally meet me, she enthusiastically says, and I naturally return the same sentiments.

We absolutely must get together again soon, she says, and I concur.

The mother of the bride takes us by the arm and graciously introduces us to a few other guests: this is Mrs So-and-So, Director General of Such-and-Such Bank; Mr So-and-So, Chairman of the Romanian Institute of City Planning; Mrs So-and-So, Director of Detergent Company Such-and-Such, with Mr So-and-So, Chairman of the Liberal Party of Transylvania. I can't help but recall how Mémé loved to mock such people who always try to hide their likely lowly origins by adopting a somewhat antiquated, ornate manner of speech. 'She's collecting a bunch of specimens *sans savoir-vivre*, and has amassed an entire insectarium,' commented her second husband.

'Here we have a pinot noir, the absolute finest to be had from the DRC,' a corpulent host, probably the best man, shouts out, 'that is, the Domaine de la Romanée-Conti which boasts a 1,500-year history. We're opening a magnum, vintage 1945.'

The society guests let out sighs, oohs, aahs and whistles to convey how impressed they are, and the chubby best man declares that he first discovered the noble juice of these French vines as an investment opportunity a few years ago, 'but today I'm opening my cellar for you all.' As he begins to pour, he continues, 'This is a *real* fine dinner wine, almost wasted on us poor fools, but give just a little to everyone, so there's enough to go around.' And with this famous saying from long ago—when people practically stood on top of one another to queue up in front of the local shop for goods that weren't there—mocking laughter runs through the crowd. Indeed, the large bottle soon turns into a sparkling red fountain, bursting with ruby, garnet and porphyry-tinted hues, smooth, elegant, noble, with a concentrated body, hefty, with a long-lasting finish. Ladies in light-coloured gowns shriek as if spattered by the the feast-day blood of St Bartholomew. 'You ass,' cries one of the guests after spitting out his first sip, 'you've been had, this is counterfeit dreck!'

The mother of the bride deftly directs us to a table near the bride and groom, near her neighbours from back in the village. Their cheerful countenances betray the fact that her use of the term 'neighbours' is a euphemism for the simple folk who live in the small houses bordering the gated community where the villas of the nouveau riche are sprouting up. She promises to find us a better table before taking off.

Our greetings are drowned out by still another round of shouting, as a fat woman appears above Flavian's head, kept aloft by a bunch of arms held high. She reminds me of the Niki de Saint Phalle guardian-angel sculpture installed on the ceiling of Zurich's main train station, and if I ever have to walk under that dubious work of art surrounded by blue ticket machines again, I'm sure this fat aunt's shrill cries echoing through Mogosoaia Palace will spring to mind, 'You animal, you animal—you animals!'

Warm air pours in through a window someone has just opened, making my low-backed dress stick to my skin, and feeling like a creepy touch.

And, lo and behold, there he sits, right before me, in a state of complete calm. It's him! I can't believe my eyes, but yes—he's sitting there, utterly still, as if it were actually a wax figure of him.

When Flavian looks at me, puzzled, I distract him from this momentous realization by telling him about Comrade Zyuganov. The way the old man is sitting there, his posture—back stiff as a board, arms bent, holding the menu in front of his face—reminds me of our history teacher, Comrade Zyuganov.

The gypsy combo plays a lovely song, every instrument sounding like a violin; 'Take me home, oh tram,' an old gypsy sings, 'take me, take me, take me to my little house, with the sweet little door and nearby spring; night descends over the outskirts of the city; and someone is waiting for me at the sweet little door.' The fact that I feel the need to tell Flavian about Zyuganov probably strikes him as rather inappropriate, given the musical accompaniment, but somehow the backdrop never seems to fit my narratives—I'm often out of step with the times. And then I realize that the time in which I have lived and currently live is merely a poor imitation of those times, conjured up as best I can imagine them.

Flavian nods in agreement. He has a way of nodding and bending his head that encourages me to tell him all sorts of things. And with every story I tell him, he and I grow closer, he becomes more familiar, probably also because I assume that the feeling is mutual, and that my stories evoke ancient, shared memories for him, too. And so I tell him more about Comrade Zyuganov who was a particularly strict exam supervisor: when test time came, he always brought a magazine with him—a magazine that toed the party line, of course—whose pages he had pierced with two peep holes. He'd sit quietly at his desk for two, even three hours. In my memory he's always motionless, arms stiff, holding the magazine right in front of his face. And then somewhere between the dark pictures of combines harvesting corn—indeed, right amid the abundant, freshly reaped corncobs—shone his dark eyes.

He never moved a muscle when he was supervising such exams, not even when we let a raven into the room during a test. The raven couldn't fly but deftly hopped up and down the rows of desks, and we watched him, giggled and tapped on the bottom of our desks to encourage him. An expectant mood welled up and filled the room.

This time, as with every other, Zyuganov hadn't stirred in the slightest. He simply sat there as if it weren't yet time, but as soon as it was, he'd shut us down with sudden, brute force. In the shade of the open window shutters we paused, following the scratching sounds of the raven's claws on the wooden floor, looking up at the formidable, framed picture of the supreme comrade who gently smiled, his cheeks dimpled. Below, on the lectern, inevitable disaster.

'Take me home, oh tram, take me, take me, take me to my little house, with the sweet little door and nearby spring.' I tell Flavian how much I love this classic by Carol Felix which also serves as the musical score for the many TV documentaries about 'Old-time Romania', chronicling Bucharest's first horse-drawn carriage in 1871, its first electric tram line between Cotroceni and Obor Market Square, then the establishment of a more complete urban public transit system during the interwar period and, finally, the accordion-like extension of stops in the city and the adaptation of urban transit to connect with various means of transport from the surrounding countryside in the communist era. And that's precisely when this song, which only became popular later on, came into being—probably in the late sixties or early seventies. It must've been after Carol Felix's three-year 'People's Concert' tour through the Soviet Union, which we even had a vinyl recording of, signed 'To my beloved children.'

Zyuganov casually lowers the menu so I can see his face again. My dear old bank robber is seated right in front of me.

'Are you following me?' he brusquely asks, with the offended irritation of someone who feels wrongly persecuted and is trying to exculpate himself in advance.

It seems like everyone else at our table is looking at us, back and forth from his face to mine, and now it's up to me to react accordingly.

'Am I following you?' I say, chuckling, 'In light of how charming your companion is, that would be a fool's errand.'

His wife nods to me in thanks. I bet she considers her man—his chiselled face, his slightly wavy white hair with the violet sheen of Brilliantine—quite desirable.

Without letting his guard down, and keeping his gaze firmly on me, the old bank robber asks his female companion whether the stuffed cabbage is too fatty.

Better safe than sorry, she says.

The bank robber then considers whether they should order another main course. He turns to me, 'What do you think?'

'Stuffed cabbage,' I say, hoping my smile will be interpreted as the gesture of a peacekeeper, 'is certainly a good choice. What do you think, Flavian?'

Flavian looks up from his menu and hesitates, expressing a polite reluctance, a hallmark of his sensitivity when interacting with older folk. 'Hmmm, what's best, let me think for a moment . . .' Finally, he suggests they order the stuffed cabbage with polenta, a classic recipe from this time-honoured kitchen, and, should the dish not measure up, they can simply give it to us, and we'll order whatever else they'd like as a backup.

'We don't wish to impose,' says the old man, following an unwritten yet tightly scripted protocol. 'We insist,' I reply. 'Certainly not.' 'Please, truly, we insist,' and we continue reciting the superfluous yet ubiquitous back-and-forth so common in this country, 'But please, kindly accept our offer'; 'That's so kind of you, but no, really, it's too much'; 'No, please'; 'No, thank you, but . . .'; 'But we insist'; 'But we cannot ask such a favour of you'; 'But really, please, do us the favour of accepting'; 'Well, all right then, but only because you insist . . .'

The old couple orders the stuffed cabbage, and we go dancing.

'There's something I have to ask you,' Flavian ceremoniously says after our first waltz—but then we're suddenly swept into a circle of frolicking men and women who take us by the hand and pull us into the festivities. Some of them sing along with the band, 'Tonight I bought you a headscarf, la la la la la la la, now I see you without it, tra la la la la la la, if anyone else, ever again, la la la la la la la, gives you a headscarf he, as well, la la la la la la la, will soon tear it up, just like this, tra la la la la la la . . . '

When we return to the table, our seats near the bank robber and his wife have been taken. We move on and sit at another table.

Throughout the wedding, I keep an eye on the old guy. As the line dancing crowd grows thinner, I catch a glimpse of him at his table, eating slowly, staunchly focused.

8

Once a week I go to therapy. This prescribed regimen is standard, and European government legislation requires my employer cover it, with the aim of helping me better process the bank robbery and its psychological aftermath. The sessions structure my week, and, in terms of how I dress, they mark a definite shift: I wear a light-coloured, short-sleeve blouse; a floral-pattern, fluttery, A-line skirt; and ballerina flats. I'm now at least 7 centimetres shorter than usual, and soon realize that walking without high heels actually makes me go slower. Plodding forward with the determination of a woman marching in high heels but whose feet are flat on the ground, I sometimes lose my stride and nearly fall. The asphalt is hot, sun-speckled and sticky with linden pollen. Sometimes I step onto a dry leaf and look forward to its crackling which momentarily drowns out the rattling of the keychain in my handbag.

My keychain is as large as a prison guard's, because besides keys to the front door, the gate, the basement and the storage room, I also have a bunch of keys for work, three keys to our family tomb and a plastic car key that looks like a miniature coffin. With each footstep, the keychain rattles against my mobile phone and overfilled make-up case, and the only things softening the noise are a wad of cash and two cigarette packs—the one with two cigarettes left over from the day I stopped smoking, and the other still sealed.

I haven't opened it yet because I didn't really want to buy it but must've stood in front of the kiosk too long when the owner, or more likely his employee, stepped up, ready to make a sale. I hadn't actually wanted to go by the kiosk near the 368 bus stop, as it's dangerously close to Sweetie's newspaper stand, and halfway through Heroes' Park I'd already decided what path I planned to take. But then I changed course at St Eleutherius Church, when I noticed someone walking behind me, the sound of his footsteps matching the rhythm of mine. Had I simply stopped in my tracks, we would have collided or, worse yet, he could have thought I wasn't all there.

For the first time, I'm not crossing the city merely to get to work, and—aside from occasional appointments like these sessions with Madame Miclescu—I don't need to hurry the way most of Bucharest's other single-minded inhabitants rush about during the day. A somewhat embarrassing feeling of being on holiday in my own city overcomes me, and lets me look at parts of my past I think I know with the sceptical, sideways glances of a stranger who doesn't want to be recognized as such.

Instead of stopping, I pick up the pace and call Flavian, who's standing on a hill a hundred kilometres away, gazing out over the vineyard that's recently been returned to my family. So it's my property now, but not really mine, as it belonged to Mémé's parents and was then supposedly given to the son of the neighbouring village's mayor, since he was from that town, or at least the area. I certainly wasn't, and none of my relatives had deigned to set foot there ever since that mayor had risen to power, and he was now serving his fourth or fifth term. But he was supposedly very nice, and my vineyard was exactly the same as it always had been—same grapevines, of the same age, on a slope with the same inclination and the same exposure, very sunny—only the posts and wires were missing. Gypsies had stolen them years ago for scrap metal, so the vines now grow along the ground, creeping down the hillside, just as had happened to the mayor's son on the neighbouring terrain—exactly the same, nothing could be done about it, in both cases it would be pointless, but that's life, take what you get, and say *amen*.

I try to imagine my vineyard, and picture the vineyards in the Viennese suburb of Grinzing, where we'd celebrated our graduation anniversary a few years ago, because Vienna was closest for all us emigrants. 'Vedi Grinzing e poi muori,' said one of my colleagues from Vienna, who was a regular at the local winery, and upon arrival we all shouted out, 'what a fabulous place, such a stunning swath of natural beauty.'

'I love this vineyard landscape,' I had said to my voluptuous blonde classmate Ileana, whose last name had since become Rinaldi and, as she told it, was now a famous alto opera soloist in Chile, at the Teatro Municipal de Santiago. She replied, 'I'd love to have a house surrounded by vineyards . . . maybe I'll buy one in Chile.'

I remember how, towards dawn, we drunkenly drifted into a round of badminton in the vineyard, watching the almost-glowing shuttlecock fly by in the twilight, without seeing who'd served it over the high horizon of the vines. We heard a muffled sound as someone's racket hit it back, and the occasional coo of a lark, maybe a few laughs, and the soothing relief of realizing we had all come together as strangers and would now take our leave as equally cordial strangers.

I blow a kiss into the mobile and hang up, straighten my skirt, and continue my walk so as not to be late for my appointment with Madame Miclescu, who will probably keep me hanging for a bit in the waiting room, flipping through fashion magazines.

The homey scent of linden blossoms creates a sticky coating on every wall and every diagonally parked car lining the sides of the streets, sticking even to the fur of the dogs in the neighbourhood courtyards and the broom bristles of the burly street-sweeper in the yellow jumpsuit with the smiley face on his back. He's quietly talking to himself or into a headset, his broom rattling like a bass drum, stirring the dignified calm of the Cotroceni district into a state of feverish expectation. The heat has accumulated beneath the shady lindens, so I dash into the Jazz Book Bar on the corner of Dr Joseph Lister Street and Dr Carol Davila Street for a cold lemonade before going to Madame Miclescu's. I stay in the bar until Fred Astaire's 'Cheek-to-Cheek' is finished. As I head towards the door, I hear it start up again, 'Heaven, I'm in heaven, and my heart beats so that I can hardly speak . . .' I can't help but notice that nearly every moment of my life has been accompanied by music, especially my childhood. The record player in my parents' bedroom constantly played songs by Demis Roussos or Carol Felix, 'Lord, turn me into a linden blossom and cast me amongst lovely ladies.' The living-room cassette deck played more 'modern' songs which I sang along with using my own made-up English with super-long words, words so long that I had to stop and take another deep breath before finishing the notes. Back then, I rarely knew who sang what, because my father didn't want to fully label the tapes, he just numbered them, maybe to see how many he could collect—and I'm fairly certain he recognized them by their numbers, just like the old the joke about the convicts who no longer dared to tell jokes for fear they'd be used against them. Instead of telling the jokes, they assigned each one a number, so that whenever they needed a good laugh they'd just recite the numbers.

The catch, however, is that I've forgotten most of the melodies, or just remember a few uncategorizable sounds, 'Or are you thinking of a song whose refrain goes ding-ding-dong . . . gone, gone, gone, sing ding-ding-dong,' Madame Miclescu chuckles, saying she's more familiar with operatic arias than pop music.

How can it be that, ever since, I've hardly ever heard those songs again, or at least feel like I haven't? This also means I've been unable to fulfil my self-imposed duty of rediscovering and remembering them all, such a burden. 'Does what I'm telling you fall within the scope of your duties?'

Mrs Miclescu laughs.

'Fall within the "scope of my duties"? What a funny phrase! I've never heard it before.'

'It used to be called "field of work".'

Mrs Miclescu waves as if 'used to' had nothing to do with her, as if she'd just been beamed in from someplace else, utterly indifferent to any and all history.

Our therapy sessions can be excessive but usually amount to little more than neighbourly chit-chat, and even if Madame Miclescu weren't a therapist handing me another doctor's note at the end of each session with a wink I'd still come visit her, just as I'd dutifully visit an elderly lady from my circle of close acquaintances if I were unexpectedly given a holiday but couldn't get out of town.

Outside, her many dogs bark themselves hoarse against the corrugated metal fence. They're probably not the dogs I used to hear but they sound just like they did before, way back when. We talk a lot about my time in Zurich. 'Zurich,' Mrs Miclescu says with properly pursed lips—she has been there, too, and has fond memories of the Confiserie Sprüngli on Parade Square.

I usually sat upstairs, at a table by the window, to the left of the entrance, with my bank coworkers; we'd eat Birchermüesli with wild berries and whipped cream, and play I spy. 'I spy with my little eye something you can't see, it's far underground, straight below the tram stop on the 8 line, headed towards Bellevue.' And then came the questions, 'Is it paper, and does it belong to an assassinated Eastern European dictator?' 'Is it sparkling, and does it belong to the widow of an Arab despot?' 'Is it a love letter?' 'Is it a gold trophy from the World Cup?' I don't know who actually knew the safe deposit-box contents and who was bluffing but, in any case, it was more fun than our corporate team-building retreats in St Moritz.

One of my coworkers, Daniel, came from a venerable family and, just like his father and grandfather, was a member of the Kämbel Guild. Each spring he'd dress up like a Bedouin and ride through the city as part of his guild's procession for the Sechseläuten Parade, while high-society ladies tossed them flowers. Once, Daniel told me that he'd like to rob a bank, ideally the bank we worked at, in his Bedouin costume. Instead, he asked his cousin to rent a safe deposit box so he could open it whenever he wanted using the bank's back-up key.

'This is the safe deposit box of Cupid, god of love,' he decreed, offering to open it for me.

He had put all sorts of useless stuff in it—a swan's feather, a marble, a ball-point pen, dried flowers. When he wanted to impress one of his countless girlfriends, he'd lead her into the vault and open the safe deposit box, about which he had woven an elaborate story. He'd then let her take these cheap objects, about which he had also spun tall tales, and hold them in her hand. Or not.

'He's like my Dinu,' comments Madame Miclescu.

'He looked a lot like him, too,' I admit.

Daniel was my closest coworker, the one I could call in the middle of the night to come with me for a walk.

'This flexibility is a sign of my fickle nature,' he said, and I shouldn't read anything else into it.

He lived next to the Supreme Court, where there were so many chestnut trees that I thought I was back in Cotroceni, on Heroes' Boulevard. That's what I liked so much about Zurich: I recognized places I had never been to before. It often felt like my Bucharest but not quite the same—not the one in which I only knew a few streets and neighbourhoods but the one I had always imagined: my stairwell with its pent-up silence and heavy entryway door with the creaky lion's-head door knocker; the angle of the raking moonlight which cast the geometry of the street into high relief; the little starling whose call mimicked barking, all night; the engine that refused to start, its rattle reverberating down the entire length of the street; all it took was a whiff and suddenly the temperature would change along the way, the scent of a lilac shrub would send me down a lane I normally wouldn't have taken, were it not for the fact that it felt like part of the winding lanes I'd already started down in Bucharest; I went onward, through a passageway, and was suddenly strolling down the long corridor of Mémé's divvied-up flat, towards the bathroom she shared with three or four other families; taking my bath in its large zinc claw-footed tub, I'd sail the seven seas alongside the glorious Captain Botev.

We always ended up at the last stop, in Bellevue Square, and everyone agreed, 'Too bad everything is closed, otherwise we could've had another nightcap!'

On weekends I ate at Kronenhalle Restaurant, and could have sworn I recognized the people at the lively table nearby; Mémé would have recognized them and said hello.

I recently read in the newspaper that there was a bank robbery in Sinaia. One day the clients noticed that their safe deposit boxes were empty. 'You know how the robbers did it?'

Madame Miclescu shakes her head.

'They rented safe deposit boxes, copied the keys, then cancelled those rentals, and rented new safe deposit boxes right under the old ones. Once a bank employee opened one of those safe deposit boxes—you always need two keys for each deposit box, one kept by the bank, the other kept by the client—the robber used the copied key to access their old deposit box where the new customers had placed their valuables.'

Madame listened, amused. 'You sure know your stuff!'

'I have to, it's my job!'

'Your job, eh?!'

She's laughing, and all of a sudden I think I catch a certain proletarian whiff to the sound of the word 'job'. But she tactfully switches the subject of our conversation to herself and her son who she feels hasn't gone far with his own job.

'He's an acrobat.'

'An acrobat?'

'Yes, an acrobat.' She shakes her head.

'Actually, it's an art,' I say to encourage her, 'a kind of ballet.'

She often goes to the ballet. Just before our last session she'd seen *Romeo and Juliet*, and before that she'd enjoyed a performance of *Giselle* with Alina Cojocaru, 'The incredibly gifted prima ballerina of the Royal Ballet in London, who's finally come home.'

I launch into a defence plea, 'Being an acrobat is a demanding line of work requiring careful preparation. Acrobats have to be able to foresee any potential mishaps and minimize the danger, all while pulling off a convincing performance.'

'Just like bank robbers,' she interrupts.

We laugh.

Maybe she thinks it's a sign of progress that I can laugh at the idea, and I go on laughing.

'He could have been a bank robber,' she says, 'it's basically the same: he doesn't get any recognition but he gets the satisfaction of having gotten away.'

'Ambition is too proletarian for him,' I say, 'he has nothing to prove.'

It's clear that Madame Miclescu would have liked to have me as her daughter-in-law. And I like her, too. On one of my other visits, Dinu opens the door.

'So that's why the dogs didn't bark,' he laughs. 'Don't tell me you came to see me.'

'Don't be too disappointed, I've come to see your mother.'

I see how surprised he is, and it couldn't make me happier.

'To see my mother?'

'Yes.'

'What for?'

'That's none of your business.'

'But you don't believe in therapy and all that.'

I laugh, and he laughs, but his eyes aren't laughing —they're looking at me.

And then I say, 'At least she can easily interpret the dreams I have with you in them.'

Dinu takes a step back and looks at me as if we were still together.

'No petticoat, no peeptoes, no service.'

An elderly gentleman in a hat and a silk scarf pushes between us on his way out. The dogs continue barking themselves hoarse, following him on the other side of the fence. At the gate, the elderly gentleman turns around and jokingly calls out, 'He just wants a kiss.'

I wave. 'You're mistaken.'

'I am not mistaken,' says the elderly gentleman, raising a gnarled finger in the air. 'Am I mistaken?' He asks Dinu.

Dinu laughs, 'You, sir, are never mistaken.'

When we're alone again Dinu invites me to the Jazz Book Bar for a proper catch-up as neighbours, which we now are again, so after my therapy session I head back there to meet him. We sit outside, at a table with a round umbrella, near the next-door tennis courts. As usual in Cotroceni, there isn't a soul in sight, it always feels like an endless Sunday afternoon in this neighbourhood. The only sound is the syncopated, muffled *pop* of a tennis ball somewhere on the other side of the wall. The waitress hastily serves us, and when the door opens a song fragment comes out on a cool breeze, 'Oh, I love to go out fishing,' then she retreats to the bar.

We chat about the fat security guard Bebe, about Caesar who wants to climb the career ladder of his laughable political party, about the old fountains around the corner and about the pharmacist; nobody really knows exactly which pharmacy she gets a ride to every day in that taxi, especially since we have so many pharmacies in the neighbourhood.

We talk and talk and talk. We both know there was something between us, or something never broached. We both know there was something essential we should have said, or should say but neither of us brings it up, and this growing impatience feels like a long-suppressed desire, a desire that makes our everyday lives seem like a slog.

'Speaking of the pharmacist, I have to tell you a story she stars in,' and Dinu starts telling me about a film about the legendary Captain Botev who married our pharmacist Aristita. 'It was a profound love, at least on the captain's part.' Dinu will be the stuntman for the protagonist, who was once the youngest captain of the Romanian commercial fleet, in a forthcoming Romanian-French co-production that will be shot in the port cities of Tulcea, Istanbul and Marseille. But in fight scenes he'll also do some stuntwork for other characters, jumping into the water. He waxes enthusiastic about Botev who was made captain at twenty-six. Naysayers claimed he was a collaborator with the ruling party; his father was also a captain, and he was close with the in-crowd for whom he procured contraband jeans and rich tapestries from Istanbul, especially ones depicting Mozart's *Abduction from the Seraglio*.

As he speaks, Dinu touches my hand now and again, and it suddenly strikes me as small and dainty, the only bad idea being my trendy yet somehow conservative white nail polish, which looks like Wite-Out and might call to mind a humdrum day at the office. But Dinu goes on about Captain Botev and how he married the daughter of the poet Pastia, the pharmacist Aristita who was famous for her huge hats, a flashy look for such proletarian times. She refused to move to the seaside town of Constana, as most captains' wives insisted on doing, because she'd become so well accustomed to the small pharmacy she worked at, and supposedly enjoyed an ever-easier existence in the capital thanks to the growing sums of money her famous husband sent home from afar. Meanwhile, Captain Botev sailed the world's seas, charted courses over countless latitudes and longitudes, wrote a diary about foreign peoples and led his crew to safety—through maritime storms, past pirates at sea and away from lustful temptations on land.

I take a sip of my lemonade.

'A ship captain's paramount task is to have endless patience,' Dinu muses, and I nod as if what simply had to be said had finally been said. We order another lemonade.

'Do you identify so deeply with every character, since you have to jump overboard as them?'

'Of course,' Dinu says, grinning.

'And do you watch the movies once they're out?'

'Only the scenes with me in them.'

And yet he knows the script down to the smallest detail. One key scene shows the captain in Larnaca, sticking to the shade as he strolls the city during the day, and in the evening complaining that the Cypriot sun beats down like a bonfire. He walks in the shadows cast by houses, and since the houses are small, he has to stoop—like so!—and Dinu imitates him with a gesture that sends his lemonade glass flying from the table and crashing to the ground. The waitress is nowhere to be found, she probably didn't hear a thing, or just doesn't feel like coming back out into the heat of the sun.

'You can drink from my glass,' I offer.

The large glasses and oversized carafe had hidden the fact that our table was tiny, and that we'd been sitting at an uncomfortable angle so as not to come into contact with each other. I grab an extra glass, and Dinu keeps talking. Clearly riled up by the story, he rambles on, and speaks swiftly, which is completely out of character with his otherwise apathetic, aloof manner.

The bent-over young captain stays in the shade of the houses, and because of his posture most people who see him think he's greeting somebody, and will soon duck into one of the doors—the only thing missing is for him to take off his hat and smooth his hair back. But he'd never deign to set foot in such a house, no matter how hot it was outside. The massive furniture, cupboards, tables, dusty shelves, sticky cabinets and framed photographs glittering from the darkness of each room would be too much. The pictures here and there, especially the ones on display in the entryway, seem to gleam with the emotional expressions of saints or family members. Everything feels frozen in the chaos of the past, a yesterday in which we know those people were alive, and now that they aren't their images remain, staring out of the frames to accuse coming generations of being irreparably ahistorical failures.

The sunlight starts creeping over the edge of the table, and I move a bit closer to Dinu.

'By noon you'll be sitting on my lap,' he jokes.

'By noon I'll be meeting up with my fiancé,' I reply.

Each night at sea, as he stares straight up at the starry sky, the captain feels as though he were an impossibility, a nothing buried deep in a long-extinct universe.

Once home, he went to law school, became a professor, and was later granted an honourary doctorate thanks to all those exotic tapestries. But then he made the mistake of overstaying his welcome in the major trading ports. He was punished by the party's ungrateful in-crowd, and from then on had to remain in domestic waters.

One night, his entire crew drunk, he returned to the bridge and steered his 13,000-tonne tanker into the Turkish sea.

9

One time we took the train to Busteni, in the Carpathian Mountains. Dinu's family had bought a small mudbrick house there, on the same street as the the train station which went steeply downhill just past their fence. It had a large garden and three silver fir trees, and there was a lilac along the garden fence that bloomed each Easter. Dinu wanted to take me to a priest who would forgive all our sins. Isn't that what everybody wants during Holy Week, a kindly priest to expunge a lengthy list of sins? Not the strict orthodox priests Bucharest is so full of—the old bastion of Bucharest. 'But what bastion? What bastion?' asks an old writer who, thanks to the rise of the envious and ignorant, hasn't made any money in this era of countless currency reforms. 'A bastion stands before the enemy to help resist a siege, and proves how worthy its soul is by enduring suffering and deprivation. But tell me, does Bucharest have such a soul, and if so, whence has it come? The fighting took place elsewhere, the voivodes fled and took refuge in mountain caves, so that the nothing was left for the enemy here but to torch the empty houses and gardens . . . This, then, is your so-called capital, your so-called bastion, the bastion without one single attribute of a bastion, where only the present moment counts, no yesterday, no tomorrow, a city of the indifferent.'

It's a Sodom of a city—even Busteni priests said so, as they listened in, frowning. 'And whatsoever is bound on earth shall be bound in heaven: and what little is loosed on earth shall be loosed in heaven.' And what little they were prepared to do was to let us young people out on parole, so to speak, and precisely because we were young we were to be given no holy supper, only holy water.

The priest from Busteni, however, was different, Dinu assured me. Back then he spent a lot of time in the little mountain town, because—unbeknownst to his mother—he was studying with the legendary stuntman Waso who gave lessons in the cavernous spaces of a former paper factory. My mother had forbidden me from riding on Dinu's motorcycle, and he hadn't yet bought the Audi and the blue police light. So we took the train.

We got to the station almost two hours before the train's scheduled departure, so we strolled around in the milky light of the station's main hall, giving pretzels to all the beggars—'lenten pretzels' as they'd be called—and buying the wares they were hawking: crossword puzzles, almanacs and magazines with names like *The Criminal*, in which we found all sorts of things, including a sample page of pubic hair-style designs.

'This one with the pussycat would look great on you,' said Dinu.

'Not even the kindly priest in Busteni would forgive you for saying that,' I replied.

Once aboard the train, we stood in the aisle surrounded by students from the provinces who were also riding without tickets. It wasn't just the kick of adrenaline we sought, now that we'd been weakened by nearly forty days of fasting but the feeling that we were living a bohemian life, full of want and deprivation.

One of the students asked us for money for 'the man,' but collected less than expected.

The windows were open, the blue curtains were blowing and the deafening clatter of the train crossing the railway track's joints drummed an underlying rhythm for our perceptions: clickety-clack clickety-clack clickety-clack, mudbrick houses with wooden verandas, shaded vineyards, clickety-clack clickety-clack, tiny people with their tiny animals, clickety-clack clickety-clack, a plough pulled by two oxen, furrowed fields stretching as far as the eye can see, then a dense forest just outside the window, clickety-clack clickety-clack, and green hills, low houses, three people on a sunny bench by a fence, further downslope a naked child running about, and a pair of sheep. The air smelt of scorched grass and cow dung, seaweed and earth, everything a city dweller dreams of. We stuck our heads out the window and faced forward, so that the images rushing by were burnt onto our retina. 'Don't lean out the window,' my mother had said, 'if someone throws a bottle out of a train car in front of you, you're dead.'

At each station stop the pungent scent of creosote wafted up to us, and a nasal female voice rang from the loudspeakers, her echoing, sing-songy announcement sounding as if it were a foreign language, arousing a vague sense of longing.

The ticket inspector, a short man, was warmly greeted by all, and then someone knocked him on the shoulder. 'Mind your manners, kids, mind your manners,' he said, holding an index finger to his cheek, 'you should have come to me right away, as you boarded at the station.' And then the haggling began, 'Put in another fiver, so it's at least half,' 'C'mon, man, don't you have any children?' 'I sure do, and they have to be fed, too,' 'then we'll raise a glass for them at Easter.' 'C'mon, man, don't be like that, this is a season for reflecting on the essentials in life,' 'Do you see the word "idiot" on my forehead?' Someone pulled out another beer for the inspector, and from the train compartment in front of us a young man with a moustache brought a lenten pretzel to sweeten the offering: 'C'mon, man, are we humans or not?' The train pulled into Comarnic, where all the houses and trees are white with dust from the cement factory—a bright, unreal white.

A second beer was duly offered, and the man backed down. He counted the banknotes, wrapped them with his rubber band, and said to one of the students, 'I'll still be on board in Posada, but if my supervisor comes to double-check tickets, you and I don't know each other, and then it's all on you.' 'Three cheers for our man!' Everyone cheered. The inspector thanked us, deeply moved, and as he moved on said, 'Have a good trip, kids!' Once he was gone, one of the students hauled out a notebook in which he recorded their bribes, 'Fat Fane got three more lei than his usual rate . . .' They checked the register for a mistake in the negotiations. 'You shouldn't have said that, he got off too easily,' and somebody added, 'The money isn't worth shit!' 'I don't give a shit,' said still others, 'Money is evil.'

As everyone squatted back down on the floor, Dinu stood up and said, 'Money shouldn't really exist, because money means debt, and it's a debt we shouldn't have to take on.' The students hugged their knees while crouching, and intently listened to Dinu. This was back when the Orthodox Christian Students' Association had organized a famous lecture series on the topics of guilt and penance—and financial debt fell into the category of guilt. 'Guilt has to go,' the students chanted, 'No, there should be no guilt in the first place.' Emboldened by his encouraging audience, Dinu launched into theories I had just told him about the day before. 'The banks are making money from nothing by giving out loans.' He looked at me to see if I were nodding, but I didn't nod. 'So, what do the banks want? Do they want money? No! They can easily make as much money as they want. What do they want, then?' Dinu triumphantly raised a finger to underline his point, 'What do the banks want? You don't know?' I loudly got up, walked past everyone's luggage and headed towards the toilet. 'They want all of us to go deep into debt with their funny money,' cried Dinu, 'so they can get their hands on the real goods—houses and palaces, everything we have . . . They'll buy us out, they've already bought out entire countries, they bought out Bulgaria, and most of the people knew nothing about it, got nothing in return. They simply use our debt to make us feel guilty, deeply indebted, and ultimately dispossess us.' As I went farther down the corridor, Dinu's discourse grew ever quieter, the lingering clatter of the train tracks ever louder.

When I came back, the group was utterly silent. 'Money is evil,' I said as a way of joining everyone again, making a V-for-Victory sign with my hand and smiling.

I stood at the window and chain smoked for the rest of the trip. The little curtains fluttered in the wind. 'Watch out for the wind, or you'll get an earache,' warned Dinu who came to stand next to me and started smoking, too, even though he couldn't stand it. And we smoked unfiltered cigarettes, just like everybody else.

10

In the early evening twilight, as the old bank robber schleps his shapeless nylon sack full of banknotes from the Romanian Bank for Development up Victory Road, past the sumptuous headquarters of the Romanian Armed Forces, and over to Palace Square, only a few of the oncoming cars have their headlights on. The air is pervaded by the glimmering sunset which casts everyone into high spirits. Romanian writer Ion Luca Caragiale, whose portrait is on the freshly stolen 100-lei notes, put it this way, 'Bucharest's evening sunlight imbues everything with a mission, giving everyone a different sense of purpose, desire, longing.' Drenched in this light and looking like heavenly apparitions, every pedestrian starts to resemble every other. Sprightly students striding towards the Odeon Theatre are indistinguishable from the lead-footed fools tumbling out of a hole-in-the-wall tavern tucked away between fancy boutiques; they, in turn, are equally indistinguishable from all the buxom, full-lipped wives of the nouveau riches, with their ponytails, coordinated jogging outfits and huge handbags crossing the street to hit the next shop. Young priests carrying packages from the Orthodox Christian store around the corner move without moving: when you look, they're just standing there, gently speaking, their head at a slight tilt, with anyone who's stopped them; but if you look away for even a second, and then look back, they're already four steps farther away, as if they were playing leapfrog. But this shouldn't surprise anyone—it's common knowledge that orthodox priests are in much better shape than Catholic priests, since their prayers call for constant prostrations. To give just one example, the theological faculty always had the top football team. And this brings to mind memories of my own time at university, and of Petru who played offence and gave the game such speed that spectators in the small stands to the right of the law faculty had to look back and forth to follow the ball, moving their heads as if watching tennis or listening to heavy metal. After each goal, Petru would lift his shirt over his head and run blindly around the field, waving his arms back and forth, taking in the applause until he stumbled or was dragged down by cheering teammates. The shrieking voices of women in the grandstand grew louder at the sight of his hairy chest, 'Pe-tru, Pe-tru!' I remember the football-fanatics banner, too, and its slogan's gold letters which oddly combined theology and comedy, 'We're coming to conquer all—Theo Angels!'

Which church does Petru preach in now? I think I saw him once in St Eleutherius Church, celebrating the saint's feast day, but I'm not entirely sure—the man I saw was much thinner, wore formal vestments and harshly reprimanded the pushy women so eager to be anointed. Could he have actually become archimandrite? I have a hard time picturing that, but as the Gospel of Matthew says, 'There are some eunuchs, which were so born from their mother's womb: and there are some eunuchs, which were made eunuchs of men: and there be eunuchs, which have made themselves eunuchs for the kingdom of heaven's sake. He that is able to receive it, let him receive it.'

A car honks for no apparent reason, and as another honks back it becomes clear it's just two friends greeting each other. Leaning against the traffic-light pole I spot a boy in shorts—Arnold?—holding a plastic bottle with foamy liquid in one hand and a squeegee in the other. A young gypsy woman who has hiked her skirt up in the heat and is hawking bouquets deliberately ignores him. 'Flowers, folks, flowers, flowers,' she calls from time to time, while the nearby cafes and salons close their reddish awnings.

My parents are on their balcony at the Hotel Continental, watching all the moving lights down on the streets and speaking loudly into two phones they hand back-and-forth to each other, so both of them can reassure all their friends they're now back in Bucharest and they'd like to see everybody at once, ideally at one of the usual spots, where they all have the most memories—Cina Restaurant on Palace Square, for example, where they've already made a reservation from Nice, or in Cismigiu Park, near the boathouse.

'You won't believe where I am now,' Mother says in her calm, gravelly, chain-smoker's voice which helps mask her hurried manner. 'I'm on the balcony where King Mihai made an appearance in 1992, the poor dear. I ran into him at an exhibition opening in Bordeaux, he has terrible Parkinsons—and a low-class son-in-law, oh the poor princess, she really married down—and he looked so small, really short, I'd never have expected, in photos they must always put him on a pedestal, and then the way his white scarf is always draped, it makes him look bigger—ha ha, exactly, just like Gigi l'Amoroso! What? Is he still alive? What? Really? Well then, just go to our office, our girl has a super-soft touch, and we only work with full ceramic technology—no, just listen, for your front teeth you'll get a porcelain crown, it's on us. What? Yes, I insist, don't even ask. What? Oh, I know, it breaks my maternal heart, I told her she's working too much, but she never listens to me, it's all work, work, career and money—sure, I know who she gets it from—yes, I know, but she never comes to visit, and I know such a darling Russian family in Nice, they're Belarusian, the boy is a lawyer, they'd make a great match, but listen: the head pastry chef at Hotel Negresco asked for the recipe of your cozonac with lard, and if I give it to him we can go there gratis, whenever, he said—just imagine, and you know what Dimi told him? Just hold on, no, wait, I'd better put Dimi on, he's yanking the phone from my hand . . .'

The flat I've rented for my parents smells slightly of kerosine after Mrs Jeny's cleaning campaign ('How could I entrust your dear parents' living quarters to some unknown cleaning lady?'), and the TV sits atop a curvy-legged rococo table. A talkshow is on, and I spot Codrin aka Caesar, whom my parents have not yet recognized as their former neighbour, the little boy next door. The background image is a partial view of Victory Road and the ground floor of the Hotel Continental, since B1TV's studio is catercorner across the intersection. Codrin is talking about his parents who allegedly belonged to the highly educated class and were punished for distributing Samizdat. His father was sent to the Periprava labour camp, his mother to the women's camp near Miercurea Ciuc, and neither made it out alive. As he speaks, the otherwise critical TV host wipes his eyes. Then the show's second guest stands up and comes back with his pan flute, you can tell he doesn't really want to play today but the pan flute is, after all, a symbol for Jacob's ladder, and its music symbolizes the stairway to heaven by which all our martyrs ascended to paradise, and he begins playing 'The Lark'. 'Listen, Despina, "The Lark",' my father yells, and my mother walks in and turns the volume up so that it echoes through the whole hotel and out into the street. 'Listen, "The Lark",' my mother repeats into the phone, as a group of students sits down on the pavement under their balcony, the cars stand still even though the traffic light has long been green, and a convertible parks diagonally across the hotel entrance's red carpet. 'The Lark,' whispers the wife of a nouveau riche complete with ponytail, jogging outfit and huge handbag as she suddenly stops, as if turned to stone, in the middle of the intersection. The bird whistles ever more defiantly, its song reaching everyone's ears, and even the old bank robber has to stop for a second in front of the tinted windows of B1TV's studio. It looks as if he sets something down, or bends to scratch his leg and then looks around to see where the pan flute's notes are coming from. The music swells, resounding skyward, touches the heavens and then plummets back to earth, echoing a thousandfold, like fits of squeaky laughter.

The old bank robber ducks but then another old man bends down towards him, and it looks like they're chatting, maybe the second old man says something like 'Hey, come to grandpa, little birdie, coo-coo-coo,' and the old bank robber winks at him, calling out 'Come, my little feathered friend, come to uncle.' The bird calls back and then he responds to his own calls, calling out again, more and more urgently, rolling his Rs the way everyone here does, his whistles growing ever longer, lasting longer than any breath ever could.

A woman cries, and everyone else stands still. Only towards the end of the song do two young priests stroll through the entire scene; the lark's joyful song doesn't stop them—they who stop all the soul's joyful songs with muttered psalms. They walk with measured paces past the beguiling music which, given their unexpected arrival, could even be interpreted as a trap set by some adversary. Many other witnesses of the lark's song could be led to think the same thing, after the song had given way to police-car sirens, up close and loud. Flashing blue and red, the lights make the magnificent facades overlooking Victory Road appear one-dimensional, like the backdrop of an operetta in whose upper left corner I see my mother and my father exit through a little door, only to return straightaway with full glasses.

11

Instead of sticking to my colourful chalk drawing until my skinned knees had healed a bit, I zoomed off at the next opportunity—and ran to grab the hand of my new friend who was constantly reassuring me she wasn't a gypsy. 'Did your mother wear a white wedding dress, or a multicolour one?' I had asked, and she had betrayed herself. But I liked her a lot anyway, because she was so much smaller than me that I could easily pick her up, like a doll. We'd run up the stairs of our holiday-flat complex, all the way to the roof, and my mother would trail us, crying. She cried a lot in general because my father was gone—where to, she couldn't say—but now she cried even more, because of me. She suspected I was lifting my little gypsy friend into the air on every landing, 'Be careful!' she'd yell up the stairwell, 'You could crack your pelvis!' The roof door was locked and my friend cowered in an anxious crouch. I had to run right back downstairs, where I'd have been punished had I not fallen straight into the sewer drain.

In the concrete drainage right in front of the only high-rise in the complex, someone had pushed the manhole cover away; I'd caught my mother's hand for a second and made it past the hole but then teetered on the edge of the cool darkness below and promptly fell in.

Afterward, everybody wanted to know what it was like to have fallen into the sewer, especially the many mothers who were also there alone with their children. But I'd already forgotten, so I just kept repeating what I'd said before, or what my mother told me I had said.

Towards evening, after my wounds—both old and new—had been washed and disinfected with Mémé's eau de Cologne, I was allowed out again. My mother stayed by the window and called me back a few times for no real reason, maybe just to see if I was listening.

A dry branch was now sticking out from the manhole, and I steered as clear of it as I could. I counted my steps as I ran along the wall—ten—took two more, then three more, paused, and checked the little shadows left by my footprints.

I was staring at the smooth wall when it hit me. A gust of wind swept by, bringing a bee along for the ride. It flew right past my ear and straight through the wall. Suddenly I felt very important, like the whole world was rushing towards me, about to come into reach, so close I could just reach out and grab it. As if in a dream, I can still remember the joy I felt standing before that wall, all I needed to do was stretch out my hand—not even.

12

A few days later I meet up with Codrin at the taxi stand in Roman Square. I've come straight from swimming in the Athénée Palace Hilton Hotel's pool and am still out of breath from doing fifty laps, even though I've quit smoking. Usually it's an easy workout for me but today I feel a pleasantly cool fluttering sensation in my chest, and am overcome by a certainty that I'm exuding a fresh coolness on this particularly hot afternoon.

Surprisingly, Codrin keeps a greater distance than last time we met, so we don't even get close enough for the usual peck-on-the-cheek greeting.

'I saw you on TV,' I say. 'You were good.'

'I went because they'd invited the Maestro as well,' he says.

'He was clearly impressed by you.'

Were the light a little less glaring, I'd have seen Codrin blush.

'What are you eating without offering to share?' he asks, to distract me.

'Nicotine lozenges,' I reply. 'You want to try?'

He briefly thinks it over—I can't imagine he ever smoked.

'Sure.' He holds out his hand.

I give him a few lozenges without getting close enough to touch him, and add that it can also help against headaches. I think he has clammy hands.

'Are they minty?'

'No.'

'Good,' he says, relieved. 'I can't stand mint.'

'I know.'

He nods contentedly, suddenly radiating a sense of profound calm.

'If there's anything I hate, it's mint.'

'It's flavour is far too sharp,' I say.

'Precisely,' he answers.

I seem to recall that as kids we were constantly gobbling Mentosan candies—the very epitome of mint—but maybe I'm mistaken.

'I'm sorry about your parents,' I say.

He looks at me, incredulous, chews the lozenges, says a quick 'Thanks, I know,' and makes as if he's about to say goodbye.

'Are you in a rush?' I ask.

'Unfortunately I am.'

'Well, I'm not,' I say, laughing.

He pauses as if thinking something over, then laughs along. 'You want to come with?' he asks.

'Of course.'

I see the surprised look on his face.

'But I can't take you with me, unfortunately.'

'That's too bad.'

'Yeah, too bad.'

'Another time, then.'

'Sure, some other time.'

We kiss each other on the cheeks, and Codrin wants to be extra considerate, since I'd been away in Zurich for so long, 'Three is better than two,' he says, giving me four pecks. He's freshly shaved and smells of a citrusy cologne.

Halfway to the taxi, he turns around again. 'Why did you want to come with me?'

'Why not?'

'But you don't even know where I'm going.'

'Maybe you're going to your party's headquarters.'

He tries to look amused. Before waving goodbye, he says, 'It's not what you think.'

People in suits obscure my view of Codrin, who's now actually making an effort to say goodbye. They're rushing by, eating pretzels and crumpling up the bags.

I don't like seeing people in suits if I'm not also wearing a suit myself—the next night it usually leads to a dream in which I'm naked.

'I'm going to the corner to get a coffee,' I call out towards the crowd.

Codrin raises his arms high and waves. I'd have bet anything he was about to come along with me.

I stroll into the Café de la République and pretend I'm looking right past all the people who are dressed to the nines and looking at me, sizing me up from head to toe while pretending to look right past me. A guy seated by the window is fiddling with his car keys, pushing the button so the headlights of the yellow Porsche parked on the pavement are constantly blinking from behind all the people in suits hurrying past and munching on pretzels. I sit at a table by the window with a view of the crowded intersection that is Roman Square.

'Where's the she-wolf with Romulus and Remus gone?' I shout to the girl with a tray. She leans in so her ear is super close to my mouth, her long hair grazing my face. I shout the question again, trying to drown out the loud samba. She then steps back an inch, looks into my eyes from so close by that she has to squint and mouths an oversize yet silent 'What?' She has the cheerfully annoyed air that women put on in dance clubs.

'The statue with Romulus and Remus,' I repeated, pointing to the intersection.

The girl puts her hands on my shoulders for a moment and yells 'Hang on a sec,' then leaves and comes back with a coworker who says something I can't make out. She crouches in front of my chair, speaking slowly, and I nod.

When it comes time to order, I point to some random thing on the menu without looking to see what it is, and the two of them go back to work. The guy with the yellow Porsche sits down across from me. Actually, it turns out we were seated at the same table this whole time but he had turned his chair the other way—and is now turning it back towards me with cinematic flair, as if this were a cameo. When the girl brings me a multicoloured cocktail with whipped cream on top, he orders one for himself with a wave of his index finger, 'I'll have the same.' The brusque gesture impresses me but I try to hide my smile, as I know he must be looking straight at me. I let him wait two full songs, the second is a fado by Amália Rodrigues, 'Povo que lavas no rio,' which it seems even people outside can hear because their movements unexpectedly shift from sudden and sharp to languid and soft, as if they're all extras in some old, meaningful film, especially during the last line, 'mas a tua vida não'. It's entirely possible that I've misunderstood the text, or maybe I haven't understood it in the slightest, and read into it a far more dramatic significance than intended. 'Mas a tua vida não . . . mas a tua vida não,' well, what on earth have I understood of the whole thing, I wonder, as the emotional notes resound in my ear, played at such absurd volume that they start to vibrate monotonously. And wasn't she singing in a foreign language this whole time, anyway?

As I lift the cocktail glass, I see the man at my table saying something. Maybe he expects me to lean forward so I can hear him better? I look him in the eye and down the cocktail in one gulp. It tastes like the little multi-coloured candies in transparent plastic wrappers that we used to buy way back when. I always ate them according to colour—first green, then pink, then red, and so on—but Codrin who once ate a bunch of them in the dark, claimed they all tasted the same.

The man across from me pushes his cocktail in my direction. I laugh, and he laughs too. Then I get up and say I'm going to smoke. I say it silently, just mouthing the words as if I were speaking, and make the corresponding hand gesture. The man holds up his index fingers, forming a cross, and we both laugh. Then he makes a sign that I should go but come right back.

Outside, I weave through the crowd, cross the street and head towards the metro stairs at a steady clip, past the misshapen little concrete block that's always been there. Earlier, quite a while ago, a newspaper salesman used to stand there hawking a party newspaper, *The Flame*. I remember asking my father once if it contained 'all' the day's news, and the newspaper salesman winked at him and said, 'Of course, all the news stories—all except one.' My father laughed, saying there really wouldn't be room to fit *all* the stories in, and he sent me away with some loose change, 'Here, go buy some Mentosan.' He stayed back to speak to the newspaper salesman and I ran off, swift as the little gymnast who, still in her tight uniform with the national tricolour stripes down the side seam, had hopped across the border one night.

I pause at the top of the metro stairs.

The cool air smells salty, like the sea. A few old women in headscarves sit on the steps, selling stockings, flowers, little furballs. 'Hey, cutie, let me make you a bouquet of flowers as beautiful as you!' I never get past the first person hawking wildflowers. After the revolution I rode the metro a lot, going back and forth between Roman Square and Heroes' Square, running up and down the labyrinthine stairs at Unification Square to change lines. My mother liked the citizens' guards who performed checks on us in every narrow passage—she was always curious to see whether they'd find anything on her, or even on me. In the latter case, the overwhelming day would lead her to play the martyr if necessary, start over from the beginning, and switch to taking buses. In any case, she dragged me around by metro a lot, 'You don't understand now but perhaps some day you will.' But my father wouldn't take the metro with us, he didn't like it. He also claimed that the metro was only a tiny part of a much, much more extensive city branching out below ground, a veritable unseen metropolis right under us, with things we couldn't even imagine, just waiting to be discovered. 'I've always told you,' said Rapineau—my father would go to his place to watch TV, and they saw countless documentaries, including one on the construction of the metro. 'Ha ha,' Elena Ceausescu lit up with a grin, 'It isn't going.' 'Well, just a moment,' Nicolae Ceausescu quickly replied—he said it with the same gentleness with which he once pushed her into the snow while bear hunting, only to then help her back up and dust off her cloak. And the train took off down the tunnel.

After all the the back and forth during the revolutionary period, I only took the metro once more, with a fellow student who said he wanted to take me back to his place. I just laughed and went along, only to discover that his place, as I should've guessed, was in a ghostly block of flats where everything, down to the smallest detail, seemed eerily familiar to me, but backwards, like the whole thing, the reality I knew, had been flipped into a mirror image—the linden trees, the rows of empty benches, a bunch of silent women seated on a single bench, in their midst a lone man, sleeping, his paunch sticking out from under his T-shirt, and on the ground nearby an old rag doll, or maybe it was a child with a glassy, puppet-like stare. 'Look, up there,' the guy holding my hand said, whereupon a highrise landscape sprouted up around us, just like the kind showcased on communist postcards with a greenish tinge, and suddenly a smell of rancid oil surrounded us, the kind that reeks in your clothes long afterward. I can still see my fellow student as he steps out onto his little balcony, naked and shimmering, his shoulders shaking as he sobs that I don't love him.

Halfway down the stairs I pick up the smell of creosote, just like at a train station. I unwittingly let my hand fall into a gypsy's hand, 'Oooh,' she cries, 'what luck!'

'You have to read the left hand,' I say, taking my right hand back and giving her my left, a folded-up bill in my palm.

She laughs appreciatively.

'You want the truth?' She asks in earnest.

'Always, nothing but the truth,' I encourage her.

But she hesitates, and strokes her index finger over my palm.

'Here,' she says, 'see for yourself, here!'

I look at my palm as she pulls apart each crease.

'Here, my girl, have a look.'

I'm reminded of how Dinu used to kiss me, asking, 'Do you like how you taste?' The gypsy won't let go of my hand. She has long, delicate fingers, like a piano player, with dark, narrow creases. She strokes from my index finger to my thumb, as if I had clumsily made my life line unclear by unwittingly balling up my hand, and then gently traces an arc around the ball of my thumb, 'This, my dear girl, is how it's properly done.' I look away, staring at a small slit in the dark marble ceiling, which is either damp or actually dripping, as I listen to the silence emanating from the metro tunnel.

'Now I've got it, here we are,' concludes the gypsy, 'avelo bahtalo! You're destined for big things, really big.'

Then she looks up at me, and is immediately offended.

'You don't believe me? Be honest: you don't believe me? Cross my heart and hope to die, really, I swear on my children, I can't tell a lie! My dear, she doesn't believe me . . . Filuka, tell her: Can or can't I read palms?'

'She can, she sure can,' one of the old women on the stairs yells back.

I peaceably hand the gypsy another bill and head back up the stairs.

'You don't believe it, do you, you twink?' cries the gypsy, 'You can pretend you do but you aren't fooling anyone.'

Her voice doesn't grow softer as I get farther away, 'You're destined for greatness, mark my words!'

The old women in headscarves look up at me, some shaking their heads as I pass, 'The world is full of ingrates.'

'You'll do big things, very big things, I'm telling you, dear girl,' her words echo up the stairs, 'just take my word for it, you're destined to become an opera singer or something like that, I swear!'

13

I board the 368 bus and get a seat right away.

The early afternoons aren't crowded, it's mostly a few women with giggly upper arms constantly fanning themselves, and some men who are otherwise unremarkable, just quietly standing. This time, though, one of them immediately stands out, because from behind he looks like Flavian—his neck has the same shaved outline, and when he briefly turns his head, his prominent cheekbones and wide jaw are the same. He's definitely riding without a ticket, too, because before each stop he furtively glances out the window.

The bus windows are dusty, and the city looks like it would in a grainy old black-and-white film with a monotone engine hum serving as soundtrack. The radio must be broken, or the bus driver has despotically decided to turn on only the speakers in his cabin. I'd bet it's the latter, because when passengers tap his window from time to time—'Excuse me, something must be off, we're all sitting in silence back here'—he doesn't even pretend to pay any attention. One gets the distinct impression he hits the potholes on purpose, and twice he entirely skips over a bus stop.

Without music the city looks quite different, I now realize I've almost never crossed town without background music and a general ruckus. I hardly recognize the city like this. People aren't even talking, an awkward silence fill the bus. Most of the women have a fan they wave on their faces, and some sigh 'hsssss' as their wrists twist back and forth, like Mrs Jeny when she's ironing.

Leaning my head against the seatback, I watch the walls of the city's ornate buildings pass by, its lushly sculpted opulence more striking than ever: rich vegetation carved in stone; leafy vines, wreaths, grapes and countless figures looking downward; half-naked caryatids; a ram with huge horns; lions, griffins, oxen, pelicans, long-tongued dragons; peacocks at their watering hole; Zeus and Europa, Eros and Aphrodite; a cornucopia overflowing with apples, pears, grapes; more grapes and lettuce leaves, flowers; and, under the pediments, giant, reclining female nudes, their cheeks crumbling. The houses have only one floor, so are still at 'human scale', and because the road is so narrow you can look straight into the courtyards—the bus puts your eye at the precise height of the grapevines.

The scene grows increasingly grainy, such that one might logically conclude it's nearing nightfall. At the next stop the first cloud of dust blows in, 'Just keep driving, motherfucker,' but the driver keeps stopping, more and more often, indiscriminately, maybe maliciously, since no one's ever there to board. The sound of jackhammers envelops us, there's a reverberation, the potholes get deeper and deeper, we're thrown from our seats, people curse, laugh, strike up conversations. Soon everyone's talking about the 'Bus-riding pin-pricker' who in the last few weeks has apparently poked several female passengers in the butt with a needle. Was the needle infected? There were rumours of hepatitis and HIV, perhaps the pricker himself is sick. But why does he only attack young women with long, dyed-red hair? The few victims who turned around quickly enough to see him described him as young, handsome and smelling of good cologne. Maybe it's just his idea of a come-on? An attack like that can get you seven years, says a chubby woman with a fan who claims to be a lawyer.

As soon as the bus stops and the doors open, everyone steps back and waits, even though they know no one will board, and then someone says, 'Here comes Vlad the Impaler, needle in hand,' and everyone laughs. 'Down with Vlad Dracula!'

This promises to be a ride like the ones I knew in my childhood. As my Slovakian colleague often told me in Zurich, when we sat with a few other colleagues at Café Sprüngli, spooning up our Birchermüesli and fresh berries, 'People just stuck together more back there, you know?' Usually one of the others would reply, 'I wish I'd experienced something like that, too . . . nowadays we're just a bunch of capitalist sharks!'

I press my back against the guy who looks like Flavian and who's now pushing me back—if I were to turn around, maybe he'd kiss me. My eyes unexpectedly land on what look like piles of rubble on all sides but I don't recognize where we are, and even if it's a street I used to know, it's clearly gone now. Some poet once said 'There is no shame in not recognizing a street you have walked on the way back,' but I no longer remember who. I spot a woman with two children on a pile of rubble, and three of them are attacking something that bursts into multicoloured shards with an axe.

'Barbarians!' exclaims a professor.

'It's no surprise,' a resigned man says.

'What can you do?' someone asks.

'What more do you want to do?' asks the resigned man.

I want to call Flavian but my mobile has no signal.

'My mobile has no signal!' I shout, turning to the guy behind me who actually does look like Flavian. We look at each other.

Everyone looks at their phones. No one has a signal.

As far as the eye can see there's nothing but piles of rubble, holes, an endless grey, but here and there I spot a pile of rubble that's colourful, for no apparent reason. It reminds me of our old family friend Rapineau who wanted a colour TV, so he'd just covered the screen with a three-colour layer of film: the upper third was blue like the sky or blue eyes; the middle was red like the sunset or a fresh face; the lower third was green as grass. Only much later did I notice that Rapineau's wasn't a real colour TV, but no one minded because it was always on, and he even had videocassettes of ABBA which everybody enjoyed:

If you change your mind,
I'm the first in line
Honey I'm still free
Take a chance on me!
If you need me, let me know, gonna be around
If you've got no place to go, if you're feeling down.

One of the passengers bangs on the driver's cab.

'Fucking hell, motherfucker, you've gotta be kidding, you think we're idiots, or what?'

Some of the women encourage him, he bangs louder and louder, then furiously pulls his jacket sleeves over his fists and smashes the glass between him the driver. Somebody screams. The bus stops with a sudden jerk, and the two men in the driver's cab fall onto each other.

'Somebody do something,' the professor pleads. The man next to me holds me by the arm, then jumps through the broken window into the cab.

The driver is roundly defeated, and we soon drive onward, with music!

The guy who looks like Flavian lets me straighten his shirt collar.

'Please call me, OK?' he says before getting out.

When my mobile signal returns, I call Flavian.

'Tonight, at long last, I'll finally introduce you to my ladies.'

14

Rapineau lived two streets from us, was my father's primary-school friend, and worked as a prompter at the opera house—a fact that greatly impressed my mother. His odd sense of humour must've been deeply satisfied when he, the man who worked long hours in a cramped, dark box below stage level at the opera, installed an equally small yet bright, elevated glass box along the fence of his yard. This curious construction turned out to be tailor-made for the operatic appearances of the lady we locals called Sweetie who began her highly lucrative professional practice as seamstress in this very cabin, mending runs in womens' silk stockings. No one could say for certain whether the interest opera singers, ballerinas and other neighbourhood women expressed in Rapineau was intended for him personally or, instead, directed more towards his always-busy and, consequently, always-choosy tenant. In any case, it seems plausible that bringing a pair of silk stockings wrapped in newspaper in order to gain access to Sweetie could've served as a pretext for some women—they would have to wait around while Sweetie worked, and Rapineau was a carefree bachelor who always had wine on hand which he happily dispensed from bottles he refilled almost daily at the winecellar just opposite the Opera.

We'd often watch from the window as he strode up Dr Lister Street, a freshly refilled bottle in each hand. His usual light-as-a-feather gait was gone, the apparent weightless-ness that usually set him apart vanished as soon as one looked more closely. Rapineau was also reputed to be one of the first in our neighbourhood to own a colour TV, even though it wasn't the real deal—he'd just covered the screen with that three-colour layer of film. But, back then, who really cared what was real and what wasn't?

I still remember visiting Rapineau on Sunday afternoons, just my mother and I, to watch episodes of *Fram, the Polar Bear*. I remember Rapineau's worn-out sofa had rose-patterned upholstery, and our silk stockings would often catch on its rough surface—my mother had to warn me every time. And I remember how Rapineau and my mother would stare at each other for ages, until they burst out laughing.

Once, when father came along, Rapineau didn't burst into laughter. He held mother's gaze, all serious, and then, as the all-too-brightly-coloured TV behind him lit up—its upper third an intense blue, the middle red, the lower green—he whispered in a deep voice, 'Despina, darling, you have unfathomably blue eyes.' At that, we roared with laughter. It became our family's joke of the summer, 'Despina, darling, you really have unfathomably blue eyes.' Mother always protested, 'I don't, really, so just quit it, would you?'

Fram, the Polar Bear opened with a song. 'It happened at the North Pole, the North Pole-pole-pole-pole, the North Pole-pole-pole-pole.' All by itself, this refrain sparked a strong sense of longing—the kind of longing one only feels when it's become clear that one has somehow missed out on everything important and beautiful in life, it all happened long ago and is now gone for ever. Following the song, a beautiful woman with dimples in her cheeks and a feathery hat came out dancing. Two clowns danced at her side, with painted faces that might have been amusing in the distant past they were singing about, but now just looked absurd. Then came the main story, about a white bear who performed in the circus, stoked on by perpetual applause. He had it good until one day an illusory longing for the North Pole set in, even though he'd never been there. He's soon overcome with melancholy, the circus director lets him go, and our hero the bear finds himself out in the wide and dangerous world. He finds he's out of place even among his fellow polar bears who don't understand the tricks he learnt in the circus and can't even begin to appreciate them. Fed up with all the snow, the cold and the dreariness of life on the North Pole, he eventually finds his way back to his circus friends, whom he still loves and who still love him.

It was a beautiful summer when *Fram, the Polar Bear* was on TV. Sometimes Rapineau dragged his rose-patterned, worn-out sofa under the grape arbour outside, and slid the TV stand over the threshold. The electrically charged screen seemed to attract everything—'Look,' Mother said, 'pollen, dust, insects'—and when she got up with a duster to clean it off, Rapineau jumped up right behind her, urgently whispering 'Be careful going over the film,' to which she'd reply, 'As if I'd never done this before.'

Rapineau poured wine for everyone, and topped their glasses off with seltzer. Of course he only gave me seltzer, and then, instead of ice cubes, he had these pastel-coloured plastic hearts filled with water frozen into ice. I always wanted to bite through the rough plastic into the ice, because they thawed so much slower than normal ice cubes. I'd shake the plastic hearts around my glass, they'd bounce off the side and their ice core would hit with a slight delay. That irked me. I kept shaking but the delay remained.

'Good evening, my dear Mrs Despina,' Colonel Dobrescu, secretary of the Securitate, said as he arrived and the show's intro music began. He kissed my mother's hand and took a seat without even greeting Rapineau.

His aversion to Rapineau was a source of great amusement in the neighbourhood, especially since the two couldn't have been more different. Rapineau was young and stately, with curly hair; Dobrescu was rather more gaunt, and tried to hide his baldness with a comb-over, raking the few strands of remaining hair from over his left ear to his right. He must've used some kind of gel, because it sometimes stood straight up, especially in the winter, when he'd lift his lambskin cap to greet my mother, 'Good evening, most gentle Mrs Despina!'

My mother often invited him over. 'First Rapineau, then him, we'll alternate,' was her justification. 'Next it'll be the general,' said father, deploying the quip that always helped him calm down. And anyway, when Dobrescu came over we ate in the kitchen, whereas with his childhood friend Rapineau—as for all other guests—we ate in the living room.

Dobrescu, who hadn't yet started walking around with a copy of *Light*—the orthodox patriarchate's weekly—folded under his arm, had a Great Dane that followed his every step. It was supposedly from the same litter as the mastiff of Ceausescu's daughter Zoe who lived on Dr Victor Babes Street, not far from the cute barbershop filled with mirrors. My father was a regular, and I almost always went with him. Every time he'd ask the owner, 'Do you know my daughter?' And every time the barber would answer, 'How could I not?' It was their ritual greeting, and they'd exchange the words as I gazed at the many mirrors, looking for Zoe's little house, or at least a wandering Great Dane who's mere presence would betray the identity of its otherwise inconspicuous owner. Zoe Ceausescu was reputedly estranged from her parents, and had pursued a modest career as mathematics professor.

Once, years later—after the revolution—I spotted a man stooped with age walking an old dog that might have been a Great Dane, and I'm almost certain it was Zoe's widower. He had always called his in-laws 'mother' and 'father', and had arranged for their exhumation in order to determine whether they were actually the ones buried in the graves bearing their names—a point of contention for many. He wanted then to be given a proper Christian burial, 'as befit them'. I never saw Zoe, or if I did, I never recognized her.

Dobrescu's Great Dane was a magnificent beast, tall and supple, its eyes always focussed dead ahead, its heavy eyelids emphasizing the sincerity of its gaze. The noble attributes of this dear dog soon began to be conferred to his master as well—as my mother was always fond of saying, 'the devil isn't as dark as he's usually portrayed'. By extension, she implied, Dobrescu was more decent than many who merely feign decency, and whose family history would have more obviously pointed towards decency.

I don't know exactly what role the colonel was supposed to carry out for the Securitate, since he could almost always be found just walking around. Whenever I ran into him, he'd stop and launch us into a long, polite conversation, usually involving a medieval castle near his hometown. 'One must never forget whence one came,' he'd always advise, as his Great Dane stared at me with its faithful gaze.

Sometimes Dobrescu and his Great Dane were picked up by a black Pobeda sedan. The dog would ride shotgun while its master sat in the back seat, next to an armed guard. The guard might have been a different man each time but, in retrospect—like Madame Pharmacist's taxi driver—I recall it always being a somewhat absent, sullen, unblinking man. In this case, he looked like one of the so-called blue-eyed boys, an 'adoptee' with 'no father, no mother'. Sometimes I'd run into him in the stairwell, a short rifle dangling beside his thigh, carrying large shopping bags or jars of pickles. I never saw Dobrescu himself carry anything. He lived in fear that his appendix would rupture.

Then came the day my mother took ill and became bedridden. It was the autumn after that splendid summer when *Fram, the Polar Bear* was on TV. There was little we could do, we just had to wait, said the doctor—a family friend from the neighbourhood. 'How can you do this to us?' my mother asked him, reproachfully. 'How can you do this to us?' echoed my father each evening.

At night, when he wasn't sitting by Mother's bedside, he'd climb up to the roof and turn the antenna in secret, hidden by the dark. 'There are Bulgarian channels, Hungarian channels, even Yugoslavian channels,' he'd yell to her, 'just hang in there!'

This was back when Alain Delon, Jean-Paul Belmondo, Jeanne Moreau and Brigitte Bardot started flickering into our house, carrying on in Bulgarian even when their mouths had stopped moving or they'd erupted into laughter. Somehow we understood the movies anyway. 'Obicham te povetsche ot vsichko,' said Belmondo, offering a spoon to his beloved with an ironic smile. Father had procured a so-called Alain Delon jacket for himself—the kind with a lambskin collar—and it hung by the wardrobe mirror, ready for the rainy days of autumn.

'I'm just not in the mood for it,' muttered Mother, even though she'd still get gussied up for every movie, as if the screen were a window and the French film stars were peering in at her. She no longer used blue eyeliner but had switched to black which went better with her brown eyes. Having perfected the cat-eye look she'd seen on Brigitte Bardot, she'd lay back in bed, dressed to kill, and play the vixen. 'Don't you dare look at me like that,' she'd warn her husband, just in case. And then her restlessness took on a specific direction and target, and she'd vehemently demand nothing less than Rapineau's TV with the three-colour layer of film. 'Just imagine, Dimi, how everything would look with one of those!' she said.

Then, as we'd later recognize from reading *Salomé* in school, my father would find himself between a rock and a hard place, just like Herod.

'Bethink thee . . . He is a holy man . . . Suffer me to speak, Salomé.'

'I demand the head of Jokanaan.'

'All that thou askest I will give thee, save one thing only. I will give thee all that is mine, save only the head of one man . . . I will give thee the veil of the sanctuary.'

(The Jews: Oh, oh!)

'I demand Rapineau's TV, with its three-colour layer of film, and that's that!'

I remember how my father's face grew pale as he left the room, saying to me 'Come on, we're going.' We went to Rapineau's. I no longer remember how the rest of that evening was—whether they sat together on the rose-patterned, worn-out sofa until my father clobbered Rapineau, or maybe Rapineau clobbered my father first, or maybe they just sat there and cried without either of them doing anything to the other while I kneeled up front and watched colourful ABBA clips flickering on TV. They were one of the few bands I heard again later on, when I actually understood the lyrics.

If you change your mind,
I'm the first in line
Honey I'm still free
Take a chance on me!

If you need me, let me know, gonna be around
If you've got no place to go, if you're feeling down.

It was getting dark. 'See? The film can't just be pulled off,' said Rapineau in the clear yet whispered diction of an opera prompter, as he tried one last time.

They covered the TV set with newspaper and fastened it tight with tape. I think they were afraid the neighbours might find out about it. Then they picked it up with awe on their faces, as if it were the Ark of the Covenant, tear trails glistening on their cheeks. 'Come on, the show must go on, somehow.'

I had to go ahead of them and see that the coast was clear, and they followed me with their secret burden, groaning.

As I neared the tennis courts, where Dr Carol Davila Street widens into a small square, who should I run into but Colonel Dobrescu and his Great Dane. 'Is that you, Victoria?' he asked.

'Sure is!' I said cheerfully, and loudly.

'All alone?'

I looked around. 'Yes, alone.' I would have been scared had I actually been alone, even if there were nothing but the trees' shadows to frighten me. Maybe Mr Comrade Dobrescu and his big dog would be so good as to accompany me home?

'Fear is fundamentally good,' said Dobrescu, 'as it protects us from potential problems—but do you think it's good for us to be afraid of the enemy?'

'No,' I replied, 'but my mother will be worried.'

His Great Dane stared at me with its faithful gaze.

'Well then, if that's the case, we should go,' said Dobrescu, and we set off towards Dr Lister Street.

'How is our dear Mrs Despina?'

'She's seriously ill.'

I hadn't meant to blab it out like that but it worked, and we walked with ever-greater speed away from the two men and their precious burden.

'What's the matter with her?' the little man asked, worried.

'I don't exactly know,' I said, 'but she's losing a lot of blood.'

I saw Dobrescu shaking his head. 'Sometimes things just happen . . . it's terrible.'

'The doctor says we just have to wait.'

'Which doctor?' Dobrescu asked.

I think I told him the doctor's name but I'm not entirely sure.

'If you're sick, you go straight to hospital, that's that,' Dobrescu said, a bit irritated. He said it was no different in his hometown, with the medieval fortress—the country has such good hospitals. He said he'd personally see to it that my mother would be in good hands and get better.

I thanked him.

At home I stayed awhile in the dark stairwell, listening in, before going back out again to find my father and Rapineau. They brought the colour TV to our place, safe and sound, and while my mother and I watched a French movie on a Yugoslavian channel—the Yugoslavs subtitled foreign films—the two men went to the kitchen and listened to the radio.

'I don't know if I'm unhappy because I'm not free, or if I'm not free because I'm unhappy,' Patricia, a student, said in the film.

Then the screen cut back to Jean-Paul Belmondo who was about to die. Breathing out a plume of cigarette smoke and pursing his kiss-worthy lips into a pout, he shrugged and muttered *C'est vraiment dégueulasse*—'It's truly disgusting.'

'What did he say?' Patricia and I asked in unison.

Vous êtes vraiment une dégueulasse, 'You are truly disgusting,' replied a policeman.

'But that's not right,' my mother said indignantly, and began to cry. 'That's not what he said!' The next day, hospital staff came to pick her up.

'But I can't go without make-up,' she protested, and then took her sweet time getting ready.

And as I hugged her goodbye she whispered in my ear, 'You mongrel!'

15

I know Flavian's ladies quite well from his stories which are surely just the women's stories about themselves, retold. Since I know them, I can be even more precise—they're his mother Sorana's stories of his grandmother, Mami Cordelia. After receiving her stamp of approval, they are then—between long drags on her omnipresent cigarette—ranked according to the weightiness of her terse hand gestures as *funny*, *less funny* and *memories from long ago*. Mami wears a silk glove on her right hand, because she'd once slit her wrists as an act of protest at Palace Square, right in front of the Party's Central Committee. It was long ago but actually not all that long ago (Mami's cigarette draws a semicircle in the air), since it was 'under the scoundrels'. She was protesting because they wouldn't grant her a passport. She bled like a pig, having cut deeper than intended, whereupon they sent her straight to prison. 'First they shaved my head, and then they sent me off to the women's prison at Targusor.' Her daughter Sorana became her chronicler, since she never left her side. Mami's passport would've been for a trip she had planned for the two of them. Little Flavian, Sorana's son, was the guarantee that they'd return home from abroad, but then the Committee asked to speak to him (whereupon Mami rolled her eyes). But prison wasn't all bad: Mami and Sorana had finally learnt to sew, because sewing was regarded as a tried and true method for reforming women, making them more feminine, and thus more gentle, more docile and more tolerant. 'Mami, please put out that cigarette! Just stub it out on the table—it's not good for you any more, you know!'

The priest seated next to me as fellow dinner guest presses his index finger onto his plate, picking up the last few crumbs of his entrée, his mind elsewhere. He's a regular at these dinners, so probably knows these stories, and the efficiency with which he cleans his plate might be a sign of clarity, as if to all this he were replying, 'Who am I to judge anyone else? It was what it was. Let us now turn our attention to what is to come.'

'I've heard a bit about Targusor,' I say, and look up to see Flavian grinning in my direction from the head of the table.

Sorana, who sits opposite Mami and me, nods to me and continues with the story of how they got out of prison but kept sewing just for fun, for all their neighbours and friends. Flavian's biological father had made it all the way to Paris—he was the only one who managed it, who knows how? (Mami uses her fork to draw something like a hieroglyph in the air.) Most important, though, is that he finally became an architect—there was no need to have contact with him after all this time. 'He's dead, really,' says Mami. Those are her first words all evening, said with such hoarseness they're hardly more than a whisper. I see Flavian smiling in my direction, shaking his head, it's all nonsense. Once Sorana actually convinced Mami to get her vocal cords cleaned, since Mami's words sounded so warbly she was unrecognizable by phone, it was just awful. The priest beside me laughs silently, without looking up from his plate. And now Mami's slurping her soup. I'm sure she's deaf—a lady as refined as she would never audibly slurp her soup like that.

The silver spoons are almost as big as ladles, and quite heavy, the plates are almost as big as trays, and absolutely everything in this house is oversized: we all sit far apart at the massive table; the high ceilings feature stucco moulding; there are mirrors all around, magnifying the light of countless chandeliers reflecting as they recede into a distant infinity. Even the darkened windows and paintings can hardly be distinguished from one another. The gypsy waitress is slow to serve us, but maybe it's just my impression, since she has to cover such long distances, carrying such big plates and such heavy cutlery. There are even a few shaggy dogs she has to avoid tripping over—they're probably blind, since they're usually right in her way. Their occasional barks echo behind all the mirrors.

'But what about that old chestnut tree? That's what I want to know.' Flavian chews as if he weren't the one talking, but Sorana doesn't give in. 'You weren't there, you're saying no one was there, is that it? The house just burnt down all by itself?'

'There have been five hundred house fires in the past ten years,' I say. I read it in the gazette. Sorana gives me an approving glance, and I go on, 'You can't simply destroy a house that's on the historic register, so what do you do when you want to sell a well-situated property in fine condition?' The priest is listening to me, now, too. 'You move out and take everything with you, under the pretext that there's an unsecured gas line, for example. And if you're in such a hurry that you forget to close the doors, or the windows, especially the skylights, it might rain in, or birds or cats might get in, or—God forbid—burglars might break in.'

'There are criminals everywhere,' agrees Sorana.

'The house falls into decay and is forgotten, there's a bunch of roadwork, the front yard becomes a rubbish dump, the kind-hearted neighbours set up a bunch of doghouses for the strays, the rosebushes grow and grow and finally cover the entire eyesore, and then one night, in the summer, a stray lightning bolt strikes, or a gypsy lights his campfire. After that, who can say what happened?'

'A lightning bolt strikes, right out of the blue!' says Sorana.

'But there are no witnesses,' says the priest.

'They're all criminals,' says Sorana.

'And when a concerned neighbour calls the fire department, afterwards everybody can say it was the firefighters who broke the windows, their powerful hose that knocked down a rotten wall or even the ceiling.'

'That's how it goes,' says the priest, 'and then there are many witnesses.'

All this makes me think about Rapineau's house, and how it was abandoned after his death and finally caught fire one night. That struck me even more than Rapineau's violent death, which happened when I was still little, during the first, second or fourth Mineriad, I can't recall the exact date.

'What was he doing in University Square at that hour?' my mother had remarked when my father, in tears, conveyed the news. 'He must've been out and about with women.' But then she, too, cried.

Rapineau was so badly disfigured by the miners' violent blows that his face had to be covered with a handkerchief at the funeral. I vividly recall the traces of lipstick left on the white handkerchief. Everyone kissed him goodbye through the cloth.

'The ceiling of the dance hall was decorated with paintings by Mirea,' says Sorana. 'Have you ever been there?' She asks the priest.

'A couple of times, long ago,' he replies, 'for baptisms, but I never notice my surroundings that much.'

Flavian tells me the house that burnt down was a small hôtel particulier. That was long ago—meaning long, long ago, back in Mami's day. I look at Mami, who has been looking at me for quite some time; she smiles and nods. Sorana says dances were still held there in her day—mazurkas, kadrils and waltzes—under no circumstances would anyone dare do a circassian circle dance there, or the equally low-class ring-around-the-rosey. She supposedly even went there a couple of times with Flavian's father. 'He's dead,' Mami says hoarsely, and the priest peacefully concludes, 'God forgive him.'

'It wasn't a place for circle dances, not even later,' says Sorana. As a light fruit mousse is served for dessert, the conversation turns to how the city has grown. 'Only underdeveloped countries have huge capital cities,' says Sorana. 'Now they want to connect the city outskirts and all the suburbs, too.' As I explain that this is the strategy of the Three-Rose Party to my tablemates, I turn and see Flavian raise his wine glass in my direction. 'By extending the city line to cover a 50-kilometre radius, from the city centre to the farthest periphery, the more easily manipulated countryside voters will become part of the capital's electorate.'

'They can't do a thing about it,' the priest says with a conciliatory tone.

'They're all criminals,' says Sorana. Mami nods and reaches for her pack of cigarettes.

'The meal is over,' Mami says, clearing her throat, and as Sorana grabs the pack from her she protests, 'and we're finished eating.'

'But Mami, smoking is bad for you. And anyway, cigarette smoke is the incense of the devil!' Turning to the priest, she goes on, 'Tell her what you said recently at church!'

But the priest simply smiles and raises his arms, as if to say: What can you do? Things are as they are, whatever will be will be, and it's not so bad after all.

Flavian stands up and offers Mami a light.

And I begin to recount what I've read about their street in an architecture book. 'Did you know, there used to be a poplar allée here, separating the trail used by knights from the main road? The streets were full of carriages—in 1836, for example, there were 3,000 privately owned coaches but only 200 carriages for public transport.' Everyone laughs.

'Typical,' says Sorana, 'even back then, so typical.'

'Around 1836, Mami's grandfather lived near Patriarchate Hill,' Sorana glances in Mami's direction with a sense of urgency, and Mami nods. 'And what a life he lived! A life truly worth living, in a city that was, from hill to horizon, one massive orchard, a gorgeous garden as far as the eye could see. Here and there one could spot a red gable, and of course there were countless church towers, since nearly every boyar had a small family church in their garden. Grandfather always rose at nine o'clock (Mami keeps on nodding), and at nine on the dot he'd go to work. He'd come home again at two to eat lunch, have a little nap and then play cards. He played a lot of cards, often staying up into the wee hours to keep playing. But for him the most important thing was coffee—he drank enormous quantities of the stuff, and insisted it be Greek coffee, with those thick grounds, super sweet. Before enjoying his coffee he'd eat a spoonful of jam, usually rose jam, which—like everything else—they just don't make like they used to. And he'd top it all off with a glass of fresh water straight from the spring.'

'And he smoked a pipe,' Mami whispers in her painful-sounding, scratchy voice.

'And after dinner—tell them, Mami—he'd start soaping up his beard without even getting up from the table!'

Mami makes a dismissive wave with her hand and laughs. Judging from how her laugh sounds, one could easily fear it might be her last, as it's almost completely silent, except when it breaks out every now and then into a painful croak. But no one seems worried, and when I offer her a glass of water she ignores it, as if the gesture were an embarrassment on my part.

When nobody utters a word for some time, the priest says, 'Flavian is on the street-renaming council,' and nods to Sorana.

Flavian declines to say more, though, and recommends they ask me how many streets in Bucharest were renamed after the revolution, since I'd know better than he. I wave it off but he insists until everyone turns to me, 'Come on, do tell!' Even Mami wags her cigarette butt, so I recite what I read in the gazette. 'In Bucharest, 288 streets were renamed. For comparison: in Moscow it was only 153, and in Berlin just 80.'

Flavian applauds. The priest smiles and nods.

'She always participated in the mathematics olympiads,' Flavian praises me. The priest follows it up, commenting, 'Say what you will, back then school was still school'.'

'Are you finished with your dessert?' the gypsy waitress asks. I get the impression she doesn't like me.

Before I leave, Sorana comes to me and insists that I go through the whole house with her, since she has forgotten where the light switch is in some rooms. Everything is massive and spotless and smells a bit of kerosene. In one room—I can no longer recall which, after such a grand tour—she even showed me an armchair that was supposedly the throne of Charles I. 'It's extremely uncomfortable!'

'See how we hardly have any furniture? We used to have much more but, during the winters of 1984 and

1985, Mami chopped almost all of it down for the stove.' She laughs. 'She would go into the next room carrying a hatchet and saying she was going into the woods. Oh, how Flavian laughed! Of course he had no idea.'

On the other side of the house, just past the kitchen, she opens a room that isn't really small but looks smaller simply because it's packed from floor to ceiling. The walls are full of paintings, and there are even more on the floor and propped up on the furniture. The pictures are all done in warm hues, and many are yellowish, a sandy yellow. As Sorana stands amid all these paintings, I realize she is the nude model shown on the sand. She laughs and says it wasn't actually done by the sea, it was just her imagination. The red-and-white umbrella in one, for example—she had told the painter to portray her on the Côte d'Azur, and he just followed her instructions—she loved that umbrella. 'It's a pity, in a way,' she remarks. 'We didn't have it all that great because it was always cold, everywhere.'

The painter has been dead for a long time now, and she says the paintings are expected to fetch exorbitant prices at auction in England. I promise to enquire but Sorana waves it off. 'This will all be for you, later on.'

That night, I dream my recurring dream, the one where I'm in the safe in Zurich. So it's nothing special, but this time I'm not alone. There is a man with me but I can't tell whether it's Flavian or Dinu. Brimming with pride, like a welcoming hostess I exclaim, 'Here are all the world's greatest treasures!' But the man constantly complains, nagging, in a painfully husky voice (my mother's voice when she's irritated), 'It's so stuffy in here, and cramped, and that is by far the ugliest carpet I've ever laid eyes on!'

16

As if tugged by an invisible thread, I stroll the same old streets—under linden and chestnut trees, past potholes where water or fallen autumn leaves used to gather and kids used to splash and stomp around—breathing in more deeply as I walk by the walls enclosing certain yards. Behind one I detect an elderberry bush, or maybe it's jasmine, or the even more fragrant Japanese honeysuckle. I know there must be a rusty garage door in the rear courtyard, which will echo the sound of my heels and wake up the neighbour's dog. And the small starlings lining the now-obsolete rooftop TV antennae promptly chime in, too, right on cue. One's calls sound like it's trying to imitate the dog's bark, another sounds like an exhaust pipe and, as if tugged by still other threads, my shifting gaze takes in the same old side streets, gardens, houses and balconies. I hold my hand to my forehead, blink, and then a beam of light bursts through between the houses, thrusting me back into the well-oiled machinery that is my everlasting, long-established everyday life.

I'd only go down unknown streets on my walks with Dinu. Oftentimes we didn't even notice, or would only realize it as we turned back onto a well-known street, melding the current of one into the other, and slightly changing pace. Our usual gait, starting out, was almost a toddle of sorts. And we'd talk as we walked, as if our steps somehow determined the flow of our words. But really it was the other way round, because a pause or lively hand gesture not only created meaning in the conversation but also inadvertently indicated the way, so both feet and words often took sudden turns.

My sessions with Madame Miclescu, on the other hand, helped me discover how a certain rigidity could lead to loquacity. She has a way of formulating questions with so many pauses, twists and turns that I am compelled to answer her with an equal degree of digression—not only because psychologists' digressions are usually considered breakthroughs to accessing our subconscious but also because I'd like to suppress the notion that Madame Miclescu is a bit decrepit and the basis for my psychological treatment utterly unfounded. At the end of each session, she signs a new waiver, extending my leave of absence. I think I'd only like three more weeks' leave now—anything longer would jeopardize my career prospects at the bank, and I also expect Madame Miclescu will give in to my desire without requiring that our conversation take a specific direction or tone. In order to give our previous session a veneer of seriousness, she brought out a dossier she'd started, full of newspaper reports of bank robberies. The most recent was the one in our branch at the northern railway station.

'But just what is the robbing of a bank compared to the founding of a bank, Madame Doctor?'

Madame Miclescu giggles, and I'm almost a bit disappointed that a lady as cultured as she is can laugh at such a hackneyed saying. I then feel compelled to explain that I didn't come up with that quip—it was penned by a West German writer who flirted with communist ideas; his portrait even appeared on an East-German 10-mark coin—in mint condition, no less.

She nods and leafs through her dossier, a clear sign that any conversation in which a certain chapter of the past is even anecdotally touched upon risks violating her sense of etiquette.

'Have you ever been to Obor Market?' I ask.

'No.'

'Neither have I.'

We laugh. My Bucharest and hers probably overlap exactly.

My walks lead me through the Cotroceni district, from the botanical garden to the tennis courts, past St Eleutherius Church to the Opera and Heroes' Square, then on to University Square and Boulevard, and sometimes through Cismigiu Park and the old city centre, where bars and dance clubs have sprouted up in superficially renovated yet still-dilapidated buildings.

'A balcony could fall on your head over there,' Madame Miclescu notes in the alarmist tone peculiar to my parents' generation.

Then she puts away her dossier—surely my parents are proud of me and my career, she says. And I dismiss that with a wave, of course, saying everyone has to find some kind of employment, and for me it was this. 'But why not chess?' she asks, adding that she'd always thought I would become world champion.

This is a question some of my acquaintances ask: Why didn't I pursue chess? My newer acquaintances are amazed at the idea I ever played chess at all, because my open, helpful manner and stewardess-like facade don't exactly correspond to people's usual idea of a chess player who is usually quiet and introverted. But the *sine qua non* of every successful actor, an iron-clad memory, is something I've always had—and was happy to prove publicly. Back when I was in primary school, I noted every family friend's date of birth, telephone number, and, when relevant, license plate.

'C'mon, ask me,' I'd nag my mother when we had guests. She would then point to one of the guests.

'Raluca?'

'17/11/1944, 369465, 1-B-3907.'

'Bianca?'

'7/10/1945, 332775, 8-B-5486.'

'Marius?'

'22/05/1943, and also 332775 and 8-B-5486.'

'This girl is going to become an agent for the Securitate,' mother would say. The guests laughed and said, 'We're screwed.'

My mother could've said having a good memory ran in the family—my father could remember all his patients' X-rays, and even those of Mother's patients.

'Which Sorin, the one who brings me cigarettes?'

'What do you mean which Sorin? The 27-year-old with tooth 27, mesial: C1, tooth 36, distal: C2, tooth 35, distal: C3, tooth 26, distal: C4.'

'Got it,' my mother replied, 'now I know the one.'

But they both pretended I was the only one with a good memory.

They appreciated it most of all when we rode the bus into the city centre and I noticed the number and location of the holes made by the ticket-cancelling machine, which depended on the vehicle identification number of that specific bus. Over time I started carrying a stack of differently cancelled bus tickets, held together with a rubber band, which I could use for the journey. We called them 'lucky tickets'.

'Just hold them with two fingers, please,' I begged my amused parents, 'these are my lucky tickets.'

Once my father and I played a trick on my mother. When the ticket-checkers boarded—six huge, fierce-looking gypsies with clenched fists—I feigned worry and asked my parents, 'What number was this bus, 21-B-5987 or 5978?'

'I think it's 5978,' said my father.

'Are you sure?' I asked, anxious.

'I don't know,' my father said. 'Do you remember, dear?'

My mother grew pale.

'I don't know, Dimi, I thought Victoria was keeping track.'

There was a scuffle by one of the doors, and a woman screamed.

'Get out, you beasts,' someone shouted. 'Out with you!'

'Get out,' my mother shouted. 'Out!'

Father laughed. The ticket-checkers were kicked out of the bus, and Mother never believed us when we said it was a joke, that we'd never been in any in danger.

But I also remembered names and concepts I didn't understand. For example, I could repeat the play-by-play of an FC Rapid match I had heard on the radio, and even imitate the commentator at key points in the action. 'Good thing I wasn't there to hear him, that beast,' said Father, 'he was against Rapid'.

But sometimes I doubted whether having a good memory was any advantage.

'You don't have to remember everything,' Father said when he saw me bent over my Russian textbook. He'd had eight years of Russian in school, and didn't remember a single word.

Then from time to time he'd take my history book, leaf through it and toss it to the floor, laughing, 'How can anybody remember all this?' He himself had no head for history.

Sometimes, however, even a quick glance at a page of some book was enough, and I'd remember everything, against my will.

And then it just so happened that our history teacher, Comrade Zyuganov, suspected some of us were cribbing from one another during class exams. On exam day he would show up with a magazine from which he had cut two peepholes. It was supposed to look as if he was relaxed, just calmly reading, but he knew we had long since noticed his peep holes, and didn't 'dare make a move', as he was fond of saying. It seemed to us as though he were looking not at us but through us with his rigid gaze, which was no less creepy. His magazine was packed with articles on the previous year's harvests and dark pictures of tractors and combine harvesters, but then one day I discovered this wonderful board with 64 squares.

As soon as I finished my exam I would look straight ahead at our Comrade, and he would ask me to turn it in and leave the room. But for the most part he stayed utterly still, his arms bent and raised, the magazine in front of his face. What had started as a dare to stare at our comrade for as long as possible somehow became a pastime—and because I could neither move nor look left or right, lest I be suspected of cheating, I looked straight at the magazine of our comrade, dead ahead of me, and even read an article here and there, since the text was large enough and I sat in the second row. And so one day I spotted this splendid picture of a game board, just above the title, 'Kasparov Triumphs in Tournament', followed by text that read like some secret code, '1. D2-d4 d7-d5 2. c2-c4 c7-c6 3. Nb1-c3 Ng8-f6 4. E2-e3 e7-e6 5. Ng1-f3 Nb8-d76. Bf1-d3 d5×c4 7. Bd3×c4 b7-b5.'

Of course, I couldn't possibly have noticed all this at the time, and I admit to having supplemented my memory with knowledge acquired after the fact—in this case, the so-called Slav defence, a closed-game opening that became a specialty of my childhood best friend and future chess adversary, Doina.

I took a liking to the Sicilian defence. When I started playing, at least, it was because of its sunny name, which gave me the perfect excuse to tell my chess teacher, the great Anton Pirgu, about Mémé's big sister Smaranda. After the war she stayed in the Vatican with a friend who was nuncio, and whose marriage proposal she later accepted. They went to Sicily together, and moved into his family's castle in Taormina but lived in only seven of its rooms. They didn't set foot in the rest of it—they just covered the gorgeous furniture with a bunch of white sheets and closed the doors. 'I'd never want to live in such a ghostly castle,' Mémé said whenever the subject came up.

'I would,' said Mr Pirgu.

He was a petit, rail-thin man—'A reed in a landscape' as my mother put it—but had a thick, black beard. As he sat at the chess board, the ends of his beard flowed over his bishop, king and queen, and clear across to the other bishop, so it seemed to me as if the opposing troops were marching out of a magical forest.

'He's shameless,' I heard my mother tell a friend, 'and fleeces us with each lesson but I want her to to learn everything people used to learn—ballet, tennis and chess. No swimming, we've cut that out since she's prone to fungal infections, and no piano, since even the smallest earthquake would send us crashing through the floor, down into the General's flat.'

I would sit in my room for hours studying chess books. I'd stick a kneaded eraser onto the light bulb of my desk lamp which would be my timer—I'd read until the eraser heated up, slid down and fell off. Then I'd press my index finger into the hot rubber and recite everything I'd just learnt by heart. I started out doing the lessons I had been assigned, and then tackled additional tasks on my own, like the ones in the back of the book. I'd estimate how much a wrong move would cost, or what advantage the right move would give me, because that would etch it into my oh-so-ambitious chess-player's mind. And then I'd press into the eraser again from below, using my index finger to push it up the bulb until it began to verge onto the other side, melting and sliding down again, and I'd repeat in a menacing tone, '1. f2-f4 e7-e5 2. f4×e5 d7-d6 3. e5×d6 Bf8×d6 4. Nb1-c3 Qd8-h4+ 5. g2-g3 Qh4×g3+ 6. h2×g3 Bd6×g3#!'

I had a chessboard, although the pieces were a bit too big for it, so I often accidentally knocked over other pieces on my first moves, and consequently felt compelled to choose a sacrificial opening—although this was nothing like the well-paced attacks I wielded when I played the game in my head, staring at the kitchen tiles, or on the street: if I passed a linden blossom that had hit the pavement almost at a perfect right angle, Nh6-f7#. A knight endgame was what I really longed for, a slow-paced match with an equally patient and cunning opponent—a game that combined all possible games. That doesn't mean, of course, that Doina and I didn't play any speed chess when she visited me on the weekends—we did, on the board she brought with her, which was made of ebony. But usually we played conventional games, without a board. We walked hand-in-hand, sometimes skipping down Dr Lister Street to the tennis courts, and then up to St Eleutherius Church.

We'd always turn to the courtyard and wave as we passed by, because that's where her father (the famous heart surgeon Tudor Herescu), her mother and my parents would sit and enjoy a spritz while we played, shouting, 'Just stay within sight.' All afternoon we'd walk up and down the street, keeping step with each other, our braids dangling apace, sequentially making our moves. I'd start, 'Qd7+,' she'd follow, 'Kb8.' I, 'Qd8+,' she, 'Ka 733.' And if we fell out of step, we'd stop, 'Right foot, Victoria, on three—one, two, three, and . . . !' I, 'Qb6+,' she, 'Kb8.'

'But a *lady* always looks straight at the treetops,' I told Doina each time her gaze fell back to following our shadows. She would have liked to take ballet, too, she once confessed but couldn't stand keeping her hair up in a bun because it made her feel as if some super-strict comrade was pulling her hair. I replied by testing her with the trick question our neighbourhood ballet teacher always posed, 'In the wintertime, are you visited by Kris Kringle or Father Frost?' But Doina simply said, 'I'm only visited by a Nutcracker dressed like a Prince.'

Since she was widely considered a prodigy, she liked to seem precocious.

But I still recall how she was just as unsettled as I when, in front of the tennis courts one day, a woman with tattered clothes came running towards us, followed by two men who quickly turned around when they saw us. We ran home and breathlessly told our parents but they just laughed and said, 'Oh children, that's enough!'

The first national scholastic chess championship we competed in was in Caciulata. The only thing I remember is that our parents rode in the same bus with us, alongside a bunch of equally enthusiastic parents and utterly uninterested kids. Our second national championship was in Bucharest, and I won a sensational second place, followed by Doina in third. After that, the next championship was in Caciulata again, and since we were already ten we went without our parents. One night she and I snuck out of the dorms with two other kids, and ran barefoot through the darkness. I've never forgotten that darkness, it was as if I were no longer myself—indeed, as if I were no longer there at all. We ran for an eternity, although it couldn't have been all that long, and I don't know which came first, the light of dawn or the scent of incense. We were standing in front of a monastery. We went in but didn't tell a soul.

At this national championship I came in first, after which I never played again. I can't recall whether it was because of Doina who didn't want to play any more, or because shortly afterwards, amid the enthusiasm of the so-called revolution, someone—perhaps my mother?—told me I should try taking up a team-based game. So I started playing basketball at the newly founded American school on Roman Square but I wasn't very good, fouled a lot and ended up breaking a fellow player's arm.

Doina became a nun in the Stavropoleos Monastery which is less than a hundred yards from my bank on Victory Road, and has belatedly donned the serious expression of the chess player she no longer is, at least according to her. 'You know, Victoria,' she said to me just the other day, 'now I play a much bigger game.'

In Zurich there is a hill topped by the so-called Lindenhof, the city's oldest settlement, where people lived as early as the Neolithic period. It is lined by forty-two large linden trees, and one tree in the very back of the courtyard blossoms in May, earlier than the rest. Its blossoms unfurl directly above a life-sized chessboard, where generally older players move waist-high wooden pieces that are far too big for the board. The pieces are weathered, slightly swollen and cracked here and there. As I watched matches there I felt as if I stood on archaeological ground, and chess was an age-old, long-forgotten game.

17

'I'll tell you, just so you know,' says Mother, and her gravelly smoker's voice has a bitter undertone, a sign of slight reproach that I don't already know what she now has to tell me. She places a cigarette into her super-long holder which must measure at least 30 centimetres—long enough that the sharply dressed waitress acquires a submissive friendliness, and comes up with an entire assortment of dishes not listed on the menu. At this point she winks at us and my mother smiles, bursting into her merrily raspy smoker's laugh. 'Ha ha, bravo my girl, you sure know your profession.'

It's noon, almost no one is sitting outside, and at the top of the linden trees' high crowns the heat makes visible waves in the air as insects flit about, trapped in countless cobwebs. The scent of linden blossoms and cigarette smoke mix together, forming a toxic combination that tightens my throat and makes every swallow sheer torture.

'Eat,' mother says, waving the cigarette right in front of my face. 'You mustn't go to work hungry.'

When I heard my father was going to be held up at the office, I told my mother I couldn't stay long, because I had to go to work.

'I'll give you just one example,' my mother continues, launching into her discourse, 'Christmas dinner!'

I nod, and she starts recounting memories from my father Dimi's grandparents' era—memories that are more familiar to my mother than her very own.

'Mémé's mother, you must know, managed to live according to her high standards until the very end. She had gentlemen dinner guests bring plum eaux de vie and pistachios. The ladies brought Chios mastiha sweetmeats or liqueur, distilled from the perfumed resin of mastic trees, a delicacy that could be then be bought from any of Bucharest's many Greek shops. These ladies wore many layers of petticoats, by the way, and toured the house, chatting about this and that'—this little phrase is the code my mother uses to convey the utmost degree of noblesse—'even taking a peek into the kitchen, to watch the chef and her staff prepare everything. And then the children unwrapped the gifts they'd received from Father Christmas. Nary a trace of Father Frost to be found, even though this was already in the 1950s.

'Then came the starters: eggs stuffed with a goose-liver and anchovy paté, garnished with parsley; pickled tomatoes stuffed with fresh cheese; smoked beef encrusted in paprika; Serbian bell-pepper sausages, hard as wood; and everything was served on silver platters, well, everything except the aubergine spread, of course, which came on wooden serving boards, country style, and was served with wooden spoons, too, otherwise it would have become discoloured—you do know that, don't you? And, of course, each dish was enjoyed on Bavarian porcelain plates, the ones with the crossed blue swords, and sterling cutlery from England. Then came the salade de bœf, with boiled beef and vegetables, and atop the mayonnaise was a large red cross made of pickled peppers, and then came the aspics, one after the other, all jiggly: ham aspic, and the turkey aspic with bits of pickled egg. After that, they took a short break.' At this point my mother takes no break whatsoever, even though the waitress has been patiently standing by our table for a while now—or maybe she's listening to my mother, too? 'The men talked about business, the women about fashion and film stars. And then the dirty plates were cleared, and new plates brought out, with beluga caviar and bread pudding, spiral-cut lemons and butter from Sinaia, followed by a dry white wine from Posta Calnau, from the vineyards that, thank God, have since been returned to our family (meaning the vineyards she'd like to sell, if she can). And then came the fish: pike-perch with mayonnaise—but, *attention*, not the miserly ones from the Baltic Sea, rather the juicy ones from the Black Sea—and grilled catfish.'

'Mmm,' says the waitress beside our table, stroking her stomach with her hand.

Mother turns to her, surprised, and then back to me, 'See, the dear girl here knows her haute cuisine.'

Somewhere I hear sparrows, they must be in the bushes by the entrance of the Athenaeum. Their chirping grows louder and louder, at times even louder than my mother's voice.

'Then they paused again, the men played board games, the women took off their high heels and donned fleece slippers from Kronstadt. And at some point, Mémé's mother asked: "Well, my dears, aren't any of you even slightly hungry?" And then . . . sure enough, out came the plump chef, proudly offering her best: stuffed cabbage! Complemented with sides of soft polenta and sour cream. And whoever wanted to could enjoy a roast chicken or tripe stew. Without further ado, out came a veritable procession of meat dishes, pork, turkey and fresh fowl, followed by fried potatoes and an assortment of pickles and sausages—from liver, kidneys, crackling—grilled mincemeat rolls, and two varieties of red wine from near Posta Calnau, served, naturally, in fine crystal. Anyone who wanted could now enjoy a coffee, too.' My mother just kept going. 'But the women preferred hot chocolate with fresh, homemade cream. Then they went on chatting about this and that, who was with whom, voyages and holidays, until someone put a record on the gramophone and the gentlemen invited the ladies to dance.'

The waitress has long since sat down at the table beside ours, and attentively listens in.

'And then came dessert, with everything served all at once so everyone had a broad selection. There was all one could possibly wish for—cozonac with nuts and rum raisins and cocoa and two cakes, there absolutely had to be two: one for Christ, and one for the Holy Virgin Mary, his mother.'

Now my mother turns to the waitress and tells her, 'And the way people danced and joked back then, that's something everyone has forgotten today—oh, how they cracked jokes, and laughed so hard they cried. At about ten o'clock a second coffee was served, a sign that it was time to slowly get ready to go.'

The birds chirping in the Athenaeum's bushes abruptly stop and then start again. It's supposed to be a soothing sound. I start to calculate what time it will be when the sun sinks low enough for the university library to cast a shadow over us, and promise myself I'll be gone by then. I will walk to University Square, past the former Central Committee building, where the chirping will be loudest. I always pause there for a moment, and stand in front of a white boulder bearing an inscription I've never read, since the sun is always shining when I pass by, so strong it's almost blinding. 'Here one can feel the devil's presence,' Petru always said. Back then he was a handsome theology student, and I was supposed to close my eyes and feel like my head was about to burst but I just laughed, and didn't want to close my eyes. He'd say, 'Close your eyes now.' I'd reply, 'No.' And then we kissed. And now whenever someone says 'Central Committee building,' I feel as if I've somehow been caught in the act.

I dab my face with the napkin but it's starched, smooth and smells strongly of lye. Our table starts to turn in sync with the birds' rhythmic chirping, the umbrella overhead morphs into a red-white mushroom hat, and my mother, who has finally fallen silent, is the only razor-sharp contour left amid the sparkles of sunlight reflecting off the square. She calmly eats everything the attentive waitress sets before her, in large bites. And now it's my turn to talk.

I never know what story to tell when my mother is the one listening. I almost get the impression she asks only in order to prove my lack of imagination, an attribute she considers a hallmark of my generation, the so-called transitional, post-revolutionary generation. But then she sets her knife and fork down and looks at me with a frown.

'Are those grey hairs I'm seeing?'

'Where?'

'There, at your temples.'

'That's the sun.'

'No, you're going grey,' she says indignantly.

'I just got brighter highlights.'

'You expect me to believe that? Those are no highlights, you're going grey at the temples.'

She picks up her knife and fork and continues eating, and I wonder if it would be better for us to talk about her life in the south of France but we tried that last time and it only made her sad. 'We moved there too late, just too late.' Or should I tell her about what's going on here in Bucharest—about her dental practice which is going well? But she already knows. Once again, I refrain from asking where she parked the car whose keys she's left me, and what it looks like. I'd bet it is a cream-coloured Peugeot, upholstered in cream-coloured leather. Some day I'll come across it by accident while strolling about the neighbourhood. The door will pop right open for me, just like in Petre Ispirescu's fairy tales of eternal youth and everlasting life, stories where the hero returns to his homeland after a long absence and finds that everything has changed, he doesn't recognize a thing, and even starts to doubt whether he ever had any homeland at all. Eventually he comes across a wooden crate nestled amid the ruins, and it pops right open, just like the decaying door of an old car, and out hops Death in the form of a bleary-eyed hobo. And, just like in the old fairy tale, Death will give me one final, well-earned slap in the face.

My mother is eating with an insulted expression on her face, and has probably stopped hoping I'd tell her a story. I'd like to tell her about a memory I have in which she's the star, but I don't want to have to think too long or too hard to find one, so I just tell the first story that comes to mind and try to twist it a bit so she doesn't find an excuse to act offended.

I remember the way she always woke my father, at five sharp each morning. 'Wake up, Dimi, it's already five, the others have long since gone.' After helping him into his overcoat, she'd heat up some water for my morning bath as my father ran up Dr Lister Street, his coat tossed right over his pyjamas, toting a loosely woven sack with two empty bottles that struck each other as he walked. Each step produced a light clinking sound which was multiplied en route to the next shop, as more neighbours joined in, and it sounded like a bunch of masts rattling in a distant harbour. An occasional 'Good morning!' greeting punctuated his journey as he snaked through the same streets where our ballet teacher took her morning run. She never greeted anyone, I should note, but it was also a well-known fact that she knew the twists, turns and all other obstacles so well that she ran with her eyes closed.

Sometimes he came back with milk, sometimes he didn't. Retired neighbours would often bring folding stools with them, and just sit in front of the shop, their ration cards at the ready in case something else came in, maybe a few eggs or sugar. The shop was called 'Complex', and from the outside it looked much like the Athenaeum. When the doors opened, shoppers could only go as far as the entrance where the available goods were stacked. The Complex was enormous and completely empty, and one could spot swallows circling its high cupola. We kids came by in the afternoon, some of the old folks switched stools while others stayed put, and we played tennis on the windowless side walls. I remember the muffled *pop* the ball made as it bounced off the wall, one of my favourite afternoon sounds. There were a lot of tennis courts nearby but we'd hit the ball against any and every smooth wall we found, even the windowless wall of the opera house, near the cloakroom. Tennis was our favourite pastime, and our time passed best where anything could happen. Many people called us ruffians, especially the militiamen and the Complex's salesmen who were a lot like militiamen. They'd come out regularly to chase us away but being chased became just another part of our beloved ritual: ducking behind a Pobeda or a Dacia, seeking cover, and then resuming play as soon as the salesmen went back inside. We always wanted to stay nearby, one never knew what might go down.

And, lo and behold, one afternoon a truck stood in front of the Complex, with a bunch of crates carrying chicks. (My mother looks up from her plate, as if surprised.) The old folks stood up from their stools, astonished, and we kids came running. The cheep-cheeping soon filled the whole neighbourhood, and hands quickly grabbed after ration cards and fluffy chicks. Our kind neighbour, Nenea Sandu, bought three chicks and gave me one.

'Is Nenea Sandu still alive?' Mother asks, sipping her Aperol spritz.

'Of course not, you know that.'

She pauses briefly to reflect but her expression remains impenetrable so I can't guess what she's thinking. Then she says, 'May God be merciful to his soul,' and takes another sip from her spritz.

Later on, thanks to an intricate string of relationships, my father got us a second chick so the first wouldn't be all alone.

'Those were my relationships, actually,' mother interjects, 'it was my friend Mia, whose cousin was a farm inspector.'

I try to take up my narrative thread, and tell her how tricky it was to name the chicks, a fairly amusing story.

'You sure have a funny memory,' mother says, audibly annoyed, as if I'm telling her something indecent.

I vividly recall how irritated she was when we had the two chicks camp out in a large cardboard box in the kitchen. Later on we let them take over the entire kitchen plus the tiled hallway, because they were growing so big and needed room to move around. With a single flap of their wings they'd land on a chair or a cardboard box, let out a crow—a deafening crow every morning—and sometimes they'd fight, knocking over bottles in the hallway, and my father would shout, 'Armageddon!' He'd grab a dish towel and intervene, and the roosters understandably became an attraction for all their regular afternoon-film friends. 'You're crazy,' they'd say with a glint of admiration in their eyes, which flattered my mother. And then someone mentioned the Hameau de la Reine at Versailles, where Marie Antoinette, in keeping with Rousseau's natural philosophy, raised chickens—much like my mother.

I don't mention the fact that I had been part of a co-op in Zurich and had raised eight chickens from a nearby poultry farm, saving them from ending up on someone's dinner table—eight hens with slight defects, one had a crooked beak, another a crooked comb—although that's really why I started in on this whole story. We raised them on a thousand-square-metre lot, right in the city centre, where we also had a medicinal herb garden and beehive. In the summertime I walked around barefoot, 'like the gypsies'. We built a hen-house, and chirped in order to lure the chickens to take sandbaths between the roots of an old fir tree. I often sat there with my laptop and office papers. We couldn't keep a rooster because of a neighbourhood noise ordinance but that did nothing to disrupt the small group's deeply ingrained pecking order.

18

‘Is that a nightingale or a lark?’

I look up at Codrin’s kitchen window.

‘Believe me, my dear, it was a nightingale.’

Flavian’s car hasn’t even gotten as far as St Eleutherius Church. ‘Are you waiting for a lover?’ he had asked me, filled with suspicion. ‘If so, I’ll stay by the door to catch him.’

The night is bright, even under the arbour, and in such sticky heat the buzz of the mosquitoes sounds louder than the distant hum of the city. Madame Pharmacist’s flat has the blue glow of a bug light. ‘Once again there was a cracking sound as they were on their way, and each time the princess thought the carriage was breaking apart, but it was only the ties falling from the heart of her faithful servant, because everything was going to be all right,’ Codrin recites. My parents used to have a light just like that, and when they went to bed, I’d turn it off.

It's a night so bright that it could have been day. On a night just like this, I was once woken up by foreign voices in an unknown house, and ran out. I sprinted, sweating, through streets that were familiar to me, yet all in the wrong place, and I cried out, worrying that I was too loud, yet still too quiet for anyone to hear. A young gypsy came towards me from a hill, carrying a child as small as I was, yet unbelievably thin. I see my arms stretch out towards the beautiful woman and her long braids—there were red ribbons braided into them—and she smiles, takes a dinner roll from one of her many skirts, shows it to me and then throws it at my head. Her child laughs loudly, and she laughs along. It is a stone.

I cut the watermelon into four quarters and push one over to Codrin. He's wearing a white shirt that looks phosphorescent, as if we were at a nightclub. I kick off my sandals and put my feet up on the chair across from me, and my mother-of-pearl nail polish glints in the light. 'Gorgeous!' the old beautician had exclaimed as the second coat dried. 'Just like in *The Thousand and One Nights*!' And she kissed every single toe.

I eat the watermelon without fork and knife, just biting right into it, as I had always wanted to do. I heard that in the countryside people don't even cut their watermelons, they just crack them open with their bare fists. Codrin says something about the heat, and we briefly muse about how it's a bit cooler here under the arbour. Or at least the watermelon is nice and cold.

When we were little, we used to dig in the ground next to the arbour, creating veritable excavations. We were looking for dinosaur bones, Codrin recalls, but he can't remember how old we were when we stopped. At one point we'd begun digging underneath the wall separating our yard from the neighbours'. The wet snout of the neighbour's dog poked through, and we poked back at it with sticks. His name was Alard, and we never saw anything but his snout.

'Who lived with Alard?'

Codrin thinks for a minute.

'His name escapes me but he built that 40-metre-high statue of Decebalus, last King of Dacia, on the banks of the Danube—the tallest stone sculpture in Europe.'

Supposedly, when he was younger, he'd fallen in love with our pharmacist.

'Who hadn't?'

We both look up at the open window exuding a blue glow.

'Your father was in love with her, too.'

Codrin laughs. 'Could be.'

But he'd rather talk about Alard's master who dyed his hair red and wore black-tinted glasses. Try as I might, I can't recall having any such neighbours. A few years ago, while I was in Zurich, at the ripe old age of almost eighty he apparently married the twenty-year-old daughter of former Army Commander Banu. He fathered three children with her, and day in, day out they'd ride rickety toy tractors up and down Dr Lister Street, looked after by a woman clad entirely in black except for a short white apron. Alard's master also had an adult son from his first marriage to an Italian poet who caught the attention of the media by reporting that until last year he'd neither seen nor spoken to his father for several years. Rumour had it that he wasn't even alive any more. And so a bunch of photographers and cameramen rented out Codrin's kitchen by the hour, because it offered the best view of the courtyard. 'I did it mostly to be sociable.'

But there wasn't much to see, since the only person spotted in the courtyard was the security guard who turned the alarm off when he came, and back on when he left. Even the children had disappeared. Months later, when it was already autumn and Codrin had made a lot of new friends among the press people—they regularly got together and ordered pizza from the Italian place nearby—it was said that the Italian son had finally met with his father and wanted to be left alone again and live in blessed anonymity. From that day forward not a peep was heard, and there wasn't a single follow-up report.

I pour Codrin a glass of my elderberry juice and help myself to another slice of watermelon.

'I love this elderberry juice,' he says, taking such large gulps that it looks painful to swallow. I think he's embarrassed by the thought that I'm watching him drink.

It's hot, and still bright out. Somewhere, probably in the courtyard of the veterinary school near the banks of the Dambovita, a horse neighs in surprise. Dogs bark, then fall silent again. Perhaps it would soon be day again, without any darkness at all—an intolerable idea in this heat. The sticky scent of linden coats everything, the metal table and chairs feel lukewarm, nauseating to the touch. My summer dress sticks to my body, having grown heavy in the heat of the past day.

'Hey, Codrin—I heard there was a police intervention outside the TV station after your show.'

'Did you see that on TV?'

'I did.'

'And did you see me talking to a police officer?'

'I must've already turned it off by then.' He smiles and looks away. We just sit there for a while at the garden table. I balance my feet on the chair in front of me, and try to focus on the multicolour shimmer of this nail polish I now realize I'd best remove—it has the cheap-looking sheen of an oilslick and makes my toes look dull. I have no idea how this was the only colour I'd approved of but it's also true that light tones are the current trend, everyone's nails are tinted like ice cream, or in nude shades, from dusky pink to beige, sand and caramel—and of course there's always the classic red which would've gone with a lot of my clothes.

'Isn't there anything else you want to ask?' Codrin says.

I suppress a yawn, and shrug.

'What should I be asking?'

We look at each other and it's neither dark nor light—one's vision is just clear and colourless, like a tiger sees at night. I saw this same colourless light at the zoo in Zurich, in a display case—it's the kind of light that makes everything recognizable. If I remember correctly, the display had three window-like boxes: one had an image shown the way humans see by night; the second had the same image shown the way a deer sees by night; and the third had the same image shown the way a tiger sees by night. The tiger can see just as well at night as it can by day, that was the idea.

'The way you're looking at me, you look like a tiger,' I say.

In this light it's unclear whether Codrin is blushing or not.

'Are you flirting with me?' he asks, without turning his eyes away.

We laugh, and Codrin laughs the same way he always has: he just laughs along, to keep up.

'You still aren't asking anything else.'

'What should I be asking?'

'Well, what I talked to the police officer about.'

I say I'm simply dying to find out what he really wants to tell me. And Codrin tells me he recognized the police officer: he says he remembered him from childhood.

'He definitely had a glass eye, because his right eye was always motionless, just staring straight ahead, while his left eye looked side to side, following everything. I think now, with age, he's learnt how to lessen the contrast, probably by doing exercises in front of the mirror, so his good eye doesn't move so much. Instead, he turns his whole head.'

This reminds me of someone I've met, too, and I try to remember where—I think I might've seen him squinting at me from a banknote.

But the story about the policeman, the former militiaman, went as follows: Codrin was quite small, and the Iancus were just coming back from holiday in their jam-packed family car. They had a cassette player, Nenea Sandu's pride and joy, and as they drove home from the seaside they'd listened to Mirabela Dauer the whole way—'Te-astept sa vii'—'I'm waiting for you', for example, which was one of her biggest hits. Codrin and I sing the refrain:

I'm waiting for you
To come back to me
Because here with me
Is the only good place for you.

Then we sing it in the round, which also works.

'Great song,' one of us says, and the other agrees.

This song is supposedly the reason Nenea Sandu started smoking. But is it even about smoking? We can't quite remember all the verses but somewhere in the beginning it does mention a cigarette—a cigarette left unsmoked, on a nightstand or a shelf.

They'd stopped by the edge of the road and stolen some sunflowers. Auntie Felicia opened the little black shells for Codrin using her thumb and index finger—she didn't crack them open in her mouth, because she didn't want him to catch her tooth decay. When they reached Bucharest it was raining, a classic summer thunderstorm. And apparently Nenea Sandu said he had to briefly meet someone, so he parked on the edge of the road and ran out through the downpour. Mother and son were left alone in the car, and the rain pounded down, so they sang louder, 'I'm waiting for you to come back to me.' They tried to turn on the wipers, and as they finally started swishing back and forth to the beat of the song, they saw two drenched men with equally drenched luggage loading their car in the middle of the road. Codrin's mother burst into a belly laugh, her son laughed along and they kept laughing until he finally said, 'Their luggage looks just like ours.' His mother looked closely, and said, 'I think it *is* ours.' She quickly counted aloud, one, two . . . and jumped out of the car but the two thieves thought someone just wanted to pass them, and said 'All right, it's OK, we're going.'

Once Nenea Sandu got back to the car, they drove to the next checkpoint, where they met a guard with a lazy eye who was very nice and offered them tea. But registering the robbery report took an eternity, and it was all in vain anyhow. Little Codrin caught a respiratory infection, and the sunflowers were confiscated.

'So, did the militiaman recognize you?'

'No. Nor did he admit that he was stationed there at that time, although I've no idea why not.'

Now I know who had an eye like that. Mémé kept a postcard on her night table, it depicted Jesus Christ. It was actually a photographic reproduction of an icon in St Catherine's Monastery on Mount Sinai, representing Christ as both friend of man and final judge—one half of his face was that of the friend, the other that of the judge. Christ's face was the same on both sides, the only visible difference was his eyes: the judge's eye stared straight ahead.

'What did the policeman with the lazy eye do after your TV interview had aired?'

'Beats me.'

'Did he arrest anybody?'

Codrin looks at me. If I were to laugh now, he'd laugh along. But because I don't laugh, he tells a joke 'from before'.

'Two militiamen on night patrol see two men beating each other up in the street. One militiaman says, "Should we break it up?" The other says, "Are you crazy? Can't you see there are two of them, and just one of us?" '

19

With a bowl full of pumpkin seeds between us and a second, empty bowl for the shells, we lie on the sofa and watch the Saturday morning news. 'Hey,' Flavian scolds me, 'don't eat so fast.' I just laugh at him, because he's less skilled at cracking pumpkin seeds whereas I have what is so eloquently known as *dexterity*—I'm deft with physical tasks. I remember asking my mother when she had started eating pumpkin seeds in my father's presence. 'Very, very late in the game,' she had said. Notably, sunflower seeds had never been part of her life, not even when she was alone. One mustn't even mention sunflower seeds in her presence. I bought them a few times with friends, in secret, from a gypsy woman on Heroes' Square. 'Watch out,' mother had warned me, 'she roasts them in her chamber pot.' They were usually packaged in used graph paper, covered in scribbled equations, and there was a joke about the gypsy who warned her little son, 'Don't be so lazy, get yourself a math book or notebook and start making bags!'

'Nuh-uh,' one of us said, 'these won't even open.' So we just threw them away.

I had always suspected that the real reason my mother didn't let me go to the movies wasn't the cinemas' dilapidated state—'Imagine, the smallest earthquake would bring the whole place down'—but, rather, the fact that some moviegoers came from the city outskirts, cracked sunflower-seed shells open between their teeth and spat them straight out onto the floor.

So for my entire life I've stuck to pumpkin seeds, and as a result I've become world champ in speed seed-cracking, thanks to a dexterity which, at first glance, no one ever suspects.

'Hey,' Flavian exclaims appreciatively, 'you're killing me!'

Whenever the smell of pumpkin seeds wafted out of the kitchen, our flat felt less like a museum and more like a home—even the most uncomfortable Biedermeier chairs morphed into more comfy, welcoming seats. Or let's just say this—with a bowl of roasted pumpkin seeds in one hand and another one for the shells, I can still happily hunker down in even the tightest corner, carefree, unconsciously raising and lowering my right arm like Coppélia waving hello in the doll variation.

And now my hand bumps into Flavian's hand in one or other bowl, and it feels as if our hands have always met this way, in these same bowls, without even a shiver of excitement, just mechanically following the way of things, touching each other as we grab every other handful.

'Not so fast, Victoria!'

'Don't worry, there are more in the oven.'

And then comes a news report, one of many similar ones, but this one has been going all evening, and is being broadcast live from Titan, a neighbourhood on the outskirts, where it's pouring. A man has climbed to the top of a crane and has been on strike there for a full seven days, he says, but nobody had noticed him until just now, when it started to pour and he turned his megaphone on. He says he's had enough of it all, and is going to jump unless Blaga hurries over. Blaga, of course, is the owner of FC Steaua, a pious supporter of the church and generous man about town, not to mention a prominent politician of the New Generation Party.

And then Blaga joins the show, since a colleague from the sport division was already with him. The sport reporter says he just happened to be in the sunny garden of Blaga's villa on the Boulevard which is about to fall back into the shadow cast by the 7-metre-high cross with the golden Christ figure Blaga commissioned for his front gate. It's hot, so ice-cold refreshments are served by waitresses in white aprons, and everyone's waiting for the man of the house—the staff have already carried his golden throne out into the yard, to the middle of the lawn. 'As you can see, a few journalists have already arrived.' About thirty, the correspondent estimates, camera and sound men not included, so a rather large crowd. 'Be gentle with the lawn, people, don't make any holes with your tripods!' a security man shouts in the background. 'Please don't trample the pansy-bed again!' cries a white-aproned waitress.

Flavian starts telling me about Blaga's villa. It's on Aviators' Boulevard, formerly Jianu Road, formerly Buzdugan Road, formerly Antonescu Road, formerly King Mihai Road, formerly Stalin Street. So it's super central, coming from Victory Road it's the very first villa on the right, a beautiful mansion built in the French style. It's reminiscent of the Boulevard Saint-Germain. It was originally built by relatives of boyar Ioan Manu, back when the road still bore its first name. Later on, the grand balls of the Billionaires' Club were held here, as were the debutante balls of the 'jeunes filles en fleur' returning from their year abroad with French and English retirees. Flavian tells stories almost as well as Mémé. I can almost hear myself saying, 'Mémé, tell me about before!'

'What else is there to tell? You've already heard it all.'

'Please, Mémé, tell me all over again, from the beginning.'

She'd always happily tell me the stories again, in great detail, as if everything had happened yesterday.

'Luckily, you tell me everything, because my parents don't tell me a thing.'

'What can they tell anybody?' she'd say again. 'Those poor dears haven't experienced anything worth telling you about.'

I can still remember the deep horror I felt back when we went on holiday in Cumpatul, around the time revolution was breaking out, and my father phoned us: there was a heroic chorus singing in the background, interrupted by a barrage of gunshots. He yelled into the receiver, saying he wished I could've been born just now, instead of years earlier.

Flavian, however, knows the entire saga of Blaga's house, even what went on during the so-called historyless period. The last lawful owner, Max Auschnitt, emigrated, and the villa fell into the hands of Communist Prime Minister Petru Groza. After Groza's death it became a guest house for the foreign guests of the Party and, alongside the villa's conversion, an observation post was also built in the neighbouring History Museum. It's been documented that many of the museum staff at the time were convinced they heard the ghostly steps of medieval ancestors in those rooms.

After commercials, the news report goes back to the man on the crane. 'Let it rain down and thunder on me,' he heretically hollers towards heaven. 'I'm the lightning-rod man!'

Down below, where the television crew is, women are standing in their house robes and crossing themselves before the camera.

'These things never end well,' says one.

'May God get Mr Blaga here quick,' says another.

Mr Blaga is delayed, so the reporter is now talking to the security chief.

'What, exactly, seems to be the problem?' he asks.

And he's debriefed about the situation in great detail up until the next commercial break, but I stop following the story when our neighbour Dobrescu stops by with a measuring cup and asks if I might have 20 grams of flour and four eggs he could use, since he and dear Mrs Aristita want to make some schnitzel to give to the poor after vespers. He peers down the corridor into the living room, where he's never set foot.

'We're just watching the news,' I say, as I hand him the flour and eggs and bid him goodbye.

'We!' he remarks, smiling happily. 'Lovely!' Then I hear him cursing at the cat all the way up the stairs, 'Are you following me again? As if I'd ever let you go hungry!'

When I come back, Blaga is on his golden throne but our correspondent doesn't go up to him. 'Mr Blaga,' he calls out over the heads of the other journalists who are also calling 'Mr Blaga' while being pushed back by the security men, 'Mr Blaga!' The scene takes on a biblical air: soon our little reporter will have to climb up into the mulberry tree in order to get a better look at this supposed Son of Man.

Back to the man on the crane, where it's still pouring: the megaphone has fallen out of his hand and sunk into the mud below. The man stands up, all alone and lonely looking. The camera zooms in on him several times but the zoom also magnifies the dense rain drops and the image becomes barely decipherable. Then he slips and—as the TV station repeatedly shows in rapid playback—falls several metres into the abyss, then dangles from a rope halfway up. And here it comes—when the camera zooms back to this alleged desperate soul, I recognize him as none other than Dinu, my ex of the aerodynamic profile.

'It doesn't matter whether you're jumping forward, facing into the fall, or backward, with your face turned away—you have to land on your back,' Dinu had told me as we came back from Busteni where he was secretly studying with the legendary stuntman Waso in the cavernous spaces of a former paper factory. 'You have to rotate on your own axis, stretching your body as much as possible, all the way around, and then tense all your muscles as you land, so as to evenly distribute the energy released upon impact. And, most importantly, you must exhale before landing, so that no air accumulates in your lungs on impact, so it's best to scream!'

I can still see myself in the crowd of children from all over Cotroceni under Dinu's window.

'Please, Victoria, she'll listen to you because you're a girl.'

'Please, Mrs Miclescu,' I yelled up, 'they've even let Codrin come out.'

Sometimes Dinu was allowed to come out with us, and he was on his best behaviour, since he wasn't allowed to get hurt. As consolation, we let him be the first to chew our one communal piece of gum.

20

He wanted to stand on a balcony and look out onto a grand boulevard. It was to be as massive as the one in Beijing or, even better, the one in Paris—a Romanian Champs-Élysées to replace the old boyars' houses with their rotten roofs and unkempt gardens, wiping away the winding old alleyways where epidemics could break out at any moment. And so the entire city quarter of Uranus, atop Arsenal Hill, was demolished, whereupon the city's twenty-eight-year-old chief architect—whose thesis had been devoted to the 'urbanization of fallow lots'—gave her comrades the good news that they now had free space to work with, an area 'as big as Venice'.

'As big as Venice!' one comrade or another must have swooned, 'Venice!'

'Bucharest's Champs-Élysées' had been known—or, more accurately, not known—as the Boulevard of Socialist Victory. It was slightly shorter than its Parisian forerunner but made up for it by being a full 8 metres wider.

Nicolae Ceausescu never had the chance to bow solemnly down from that balcony, so Michael Jackson did it in his stead, complete with glittering white glove. This was three years after Ceausescu's execution, during Michael's *Dangerous* World Tour.

Back then hardly anyone left home without their personal copy of his *Dangerous* cassette—people carried them around just like the Chinese kept Mao's *Little Red Book* on hand during the Cultural Revolution. Everyone who owned a cassette player, like we did, would play 'Jackson Poker'. You'd take a pencil or your finger and spin the tape to a random spot. Each player then had to guess what Michael would be singing when the music resumed. After everyone had placed their bets, the cassette was pushed into the recorder and the person whose guess was closest won the round.

I never knew
But I was living in vain
She called my house
She said you know my name . . .

I had two copies of the *Dangerous* cassette. I listened to one and kept the other hidden in a safe place, in case the first one broke. When CDs came along, my father bought me the album on CD, in case we ever managed to buy a CD player.

When it was announced that Michael would be brought directly to the People's House upon landing in Bucharest, I was one of the seventy thousand fans who, under the dark of night, pushed their way into the concrete gorge between the nearby residential blocks, an area known as Via Mala. Before us loomed the steep rock wall of the monstrous building, still under construction. It, too, could have been a night of sorts—a black, starless night, behind which one would find only wasteland and fallow terrain. For the first time, I now stood in front of this building, a massif I had only ever seen at a distance, from the window on Dr Joseph Lister Street. And I probably never would have come here if it weren't for Michael.

There were only a few sporadic shouts until the helicopters showed up, piercing the night with cones of light. The crowd's shouts grew, 'Michaaael, Miiichaaael,' ropes were dropped from the helicopters, and everyone looked up to see if Michael was going to slide down to us amid the relentless autumn rain.

'Is that him?'

'That has to be him.'

But there was no one there.

We sang his songs to him, all mixed up. Sometimes a song sprang up from the back of the crowd and swept over us like a wave, bringing everyone's voice upward and forward:

And it doesn't seem to matter
And it doesn't seem right
'cause the will has brought
No fortune
Still I cry alone at night
Don't you judge of my composure
'cause I'm lying to myself
And the reason why she left me
Did she find in someone else?

And then another song welled up, initially sweeping the first one away, then bringing it back. This one was about love and betrayal, but above all betrayal, and everyone sang in unison:

(*Who is it?*)
Is it a friend of mine?
(*Who is it?*)
Is it my brother?
(*Who is it?*)
Somebody hurt my soul, now
(*Who is it?*)
I can't take it 'cause I'm lonely.

Out of nowhere the night exploded before us, with a roar and apocalyptic fireworks all around the People's House.

'It's burning,' a few people cried out, fascinated, 'he's going to burn it all down.'

The sound of sirens struck us from all sides.

There we stood at the foot of Arsenal Hill, mythical gathering place of ungodly might, a steaming mass of human beings, drenched to the bone yet strengthened, blessed by the suffering of our ancestors, the chosen few who'd experience the end of it all, the ultimate, decisive battle prophesied in the Book of Revelation. 'And he gathered them together into a place called in the Hebrew tongue *Armageddon*.'

'Michael, Michael,' we called out to our archangel.

And when the entire People's House had disappeared behind fire and smoke, someone shouted, 'Down with the nomenklatura!' Or it simply came over us all, and everybody began chanting, 'Down with the nomenklatura!'

'Free-dom, free-dom!'

Everyone stretched their arms out into the rain, their fingers forming the victory sign—much like the one democrats had flashed a year before, but now with index-finger and thumbs, no longer the V-sign made with the index and middle fingers used in the so-called revolution, since the nomenklatura's cruel, gruesome spectacle had made us out to be the suckers.

Once the smoke had settled, washed away by the rain, we had a clear view of what was once the mere People's House, and now revealed itself, in blue contours, to be the Heavenly People's House, the House of all God's People.

Heal the world
Make it a better place
For you and for me
And the entire human race . . .

A bunch of light beams came together on the balcony of the People's House, where a small figure stood and waved. 'Huuuh,' Michael shouted into the microphone, 'huuh!'

Two large screens flashed in the night, showing an oversized Michael Jackson in the red-and-blue officer's uniform of the royal guard, complete with golden cords. If you check the history books, you'll see that it was exactly like King Charles II's gala uniform, just without the fancy white-tufted cap. Instead, he wore a black hat and mirrored aviator glasses in which the entire enormous square was reflected, teeming with innumerable teeny dots.

'Hello, *Budapest*!' Michael Jackson shouted. 'I love you!'

It seemed as if, in the blink of an eye, the rain had stopped. Or that the raindrops were suddenly stuck, hovering in mid-air, just like the surrounding smoke. Dead silence. The End.

It's completely silent up here on this summer morning, not a sound reaches us up on the balcony where we're seated on rattan chairs, drinking iced mochas and peering out between the balustrade's chunky concrete pillars onto the now-defunct Unification Boulevard, formerly the Boulevard of Socialist Victory. The cream-coloured blocks of flats are all clustered together and appear uninhabited. The few passersby don't stop at the entrances but disappear into shadowy passages and emerge on the other side where there are still small houses and gardens. That other side is also where the small church from the now-demolished Mihai Voda Monastery was moved, purportedly slid into safety on squat wheels and temporary rails, to save it from being razed along with everything else nearby. Large cream-coloured umbrellas—the kind I recognize from my time in Switzerland—protect us from the sun and birds, since the airspace above the 300-metre-long People's House has become a magnet for Mediterranean gulls. They began to drift beyond their natural habitat a few years ago, and now silently yet incessantly circle the sky, scavenging the city's garbage. A strong scent of hay blows towards us from the hill, whose grass has grown taller than I. It feels as if we're on a balcony in Halkidiki, Greece, Flavian's former schoolmate notes—this is the schoolmate who got rich in Silicon Valley but claims to regret having left Eastern Europe and its rich traditions. He had made appointments all morning and then cancelled them all. How liberating it is to blow off such American obsessive-compulsiveness! His newlywed wife agrees, and adds that she found the People's House simply stunning. She loved it, she'd felt as if she were running through an installation by that famous Swiss artist—she looks at me as she says this—oh, what's-her-name, you know, the one who designed that huge room with big red sofas where the viewer suddenly feels so small, so innocent, so carefree. Being in such a huge house gives one the feeling of being a child again, it's fantastic, it makes you want to let loose. She sips her mocha through two candy-coloured straws and asks me to go back inside with her. Flavian and her husband welcome the idea.

'Go ahead,' they say, ordering a second round of iced mochas.

We're both blinded by the sun, the woman takes me by the hand, and I realize I've forgotten her name. But I remember her maiden name, Moinescu, like her rich father, whose father was, in turn, a Communist prime minister. There was a good joke about Moinescu but it doesn't come to mind—I wonder whether she knows it, or maybe she doesn't have a clue?

I had known a lot of jokes, so many that I could sit for hours on end just telling political jokes. Between each one, by way of introduction, I'd repeat, 'And now this one . . .'

'Did the kids tell jokes while you were out playing?' my mother would always ask when I came home.

'Yup.'

'And you?'

'Nope.'

'Nope what?'

'I didn't tell any.'

'But didn't they insist you tell at least one?'

'Sure they did but I didn't tell a single one.'

'I wish I could believe you.'

She scrutinized me with a stern gaze, as if to chastise me with her distrust, just in case. But that didn't last long, because she really just wanted to hear the other kids' jokes.

'Come on, tell me another,' she'd say after every joke.

'But I don't know any others.'

'Try to remember.'

'OK', I said, 'Ceausescu, Gorbachev and Reagan were flying in a helicopter . . .'.

'Is that the one with the clock?'

'No, it's the one with the crocodile boots.'

'That's an old one.'

'Fine, then how about this one: Brezhnev and Nixon went hunting . . .'

We go through the rooms at a steady clip as the young Ms Née-Moinescu takes me by the hand, pulls me past massive cold walls, and starts counting our steps only to quit counting out of excitement, wowed by the sheer scale of everything. The rooms are empty, the heavy curtains are drawn, and we wade through the twilight, crossing thick carpets punctuated by lines of sunlight piercing through here and there, hinting at some huge pattern that could only be recognized from the ceiling.

'Do you think the two of them ever had sex here?' she asks.

'Who?'

'The Ceausescus, who else?'

'I don't think so. This wasn't a flat but a government building.'

'Yeah—but can't you have sex in a government building?'

'I don't think so, because they were always in official company.'

'But they could've snuck off and had a quickie in the bathroom, just to show everybody they could do it in secret.'

'I don't think they ever wanted to be alone, they were afraid of being attacked.'

The young woman is clearly annoyed. She wants to contradict me but has no good arguments. Is her grandfather still alive? She's part of the so-called post-revolution generation, one of those who hasn't saddled themselves with any guilt but somehow wanders about bearing—brandishing, even—this arrogant air of blamelessness. And then it comes to me, her name is Victoria, just like me.

What a scandal, a Moinescu named Victoria! And she was only born after the revolution!

Right beside one of the doorways there's a long ladder. We take a few steps backward, look up and see a petite cleaning lady at the very top who doesn't seem to be moving. Victoria asks whether she's afraid of falling off the ladder but probably just wants to check the acoustics in the cavernous hall.

'Don't touch!' I whisper as she tries to shake the ladder holding up the immobile cleaning lady, and my whisper echoes through the marble hall with a barely perceptible delay, like some poorly executed lip sync.

In hindsight, I don't want to make her seem like a bad person—I hardly knew her, really—but I also figure I'm not so far off the mark when I say the young Ms Née-Moinescu was a woman who put on airs.

'You think the Ceausescus were really like that?' Victoria muses in a loud voice.

'I met them once.'

'Seriously?'

So I tell her the story of how I had been a 'Pioneer of the Fatherland' when I was little, and was chosen as one of the few who got to meet our 'supreme comrades', and how it all really happened. I tell the story more for myself than for her, as if I had to tell it in this specific place.

'Sick,' says Victoria.

Radio chit-chat floats up to us from somewhere, drifting in like a warm wind.

Out on one of the terraces, Victoria asks me to take her picture. She hands me her camera, climbs up to the parapet and holds onto the corner pillar. As if nudged by the voices on the radio, whose volume goes up and down like a random gust of wind, I ask her what she wants in the photo. Herself and the city, she says in the kind of tone that implies that should've been obvious.

But my question was spot on, because from this balcony you don't really see much of anything, just a backdrop of boring, cream-coloured residential blocks.

'Just jump already,' says the devil but I know the answer, 'Thou shalt not tempt the Lord thy God.'

Something emerges from the light blue haze, appearing a bit like the Alps as seen from Zurich, across the lake. I press down.

21

I became a 'Pioneer of the Fatherland' when I was ten years old, on a cold autumn day, or maybe a cold spring day—in any case, it was cold, and we weren't allowed to put a jacket on over our snow-white pioneers' blouses so they wouldn't look all wrinkled at the big ceremony. The day had begun badly, because my red carnation had been swiftly beheaded by one of my fellow pioneers. He was small and graceful but his parents sent him to karate. He was showing off his flying kick, and my carnation happened to be in the way. I was left with only the stalk, so I could've duelled with a fellow pioneer who also had only the stalk but everyone else's carnations were still intact.

So I had to stand in the last row when we lined up for the patriotic song, hidden back where nobody would see that I didn't have a flower. It wouldn't have been so bad had the walls of the old prison not been so cold—the celebration was held in the ruins of Doftana prison, not far from Bucharest, where Ceausescu and his predecessor Gheorghiu-Dej had been imprisoned, as had the grandfather of one of my schoolmates, a fat blonde named Ileana. She was named after Princess Ileana of Romania, with whom her grandfather—despite his perfunctory communism, or perhaps precisely because of it—supposedly had an affair.

After a dress rehearsal of the ceremony in which we all received our official red ties, we were allowed to break for a short picnic on the lawn. The ground was cold and wet, and we spent so much time in vain, and covered so much ground searching for a suitable spot to sit, that we unexpectedly found ourselves back inside the prison walls, in a cellblock. We played catch, and then hide-and-seek, until Virgil called us. He had found iron handcuffs chained to the wall in one of the cells.

'Do you guys think they're real?'

We took a closer look—they seemed pretty ancient, given how rusty they were.

At the time we were all entranced by Alexandre Dumas's novel *The Count of Monte Cristo*, and between classes we'd excitedly discuss the adventurous escape of the innocent prisoner who then appeared before his tormentors as the avenging angel. These discussions usually escalated into major disagreements, because each of us had our own ideas about how the story went, which led us to deduce that everyone else somehow had the wrong idea. Dumas books had to be reserved from the school library far in advance. Their good condition attested to the high value their readers ascribed to them. When my turn came, I protected the books in my own special newspaper dust-jacket, and paged through it as if poring over a priceless manuscript. But even then I couldn't help scraping the little bits of wood out of the paper, and as those bits came off the surface a word here and a word there invariably came with them, unintentionally making minor changes to the book's plot. Consequently, I left my own impression on these heroic stories, as I liked to imagine during the many nights spent secretly reading by flashlight under the blankets. The text on the other side of the page sometimes came through the brown paper which made reading it much more difficult. The tedious process of deciphering each word made me feel like the first-ever, specially chosen reader. Sometimes I even tried to read the other side without turning the page, which meant reading in reverse, in order to anticipate the thickening plot. I always read in secret, hiding the books from my mother who didn't want me to bring any library books home—you never knew whether the previous reader had succumbed to tuberculosis, or some other contagion. For every page I read, I was ready to pay the highest price, my very life, which I figured was what made me truly worthy of encountering the heroes and martyrs in such stories.

'Let's play with the handcuffs,' someone suggested, and then everyone wanted to be the noble inmate. As fate would have it, however, only Virgil's delicate wrists fit into the already closed handcuffs.

And who could the rest of us be? We all disagreed.

'You all can be my my guards.'

But that was no fun, so we decided to be his evil torturers.

'And then we can switch,' said Virgil in a conciliatory tone, as we left him in his cell and went out to fetch our instruments of torture—pointy sticks to poke and prod him, big stones to smash his bones, and then all sorts of wildflowers we could say were poisonous, and I even found a snakeskin which excited us all. We held it up against the weak sun, studying its fine patterns until our comrade teacher found us. 'Can't you hear when someone's calling you?'

She was out of breath and close to tears. I don't know why the ceremony had to start so punctually, there was no one out in this wilderness but us, her and a comrade inspector who was quietly playing tric-trac with the bus driver. 'Go on, run to the entrance wall and line up, quick,' she commanded, but on the way back we remembered Virgil. And then something funny happened—we had forgotten which cell he was in, and right before our eyes the cellblock grew increasingly labyrinthine. We wanted to call out to Virgil but our comrade teacher was afraid the comrade inspector would hear us and realize that not everything was going according to plan, and that we weren't a collective worthy of wearing the red tie but just 'a bunch of wretched losers'. 'Go now, but keep quiet,' she finally said, and we ran from cell to cell whispering, 'Virgil, are you there?', only to then shout loudly over the walls, 'He's not here,' and then, 'Not here, either!'

As I remember it, all of a sudden it was dark, clouds had blown in or night had unexpectedly fallen. When we found Virgil, we noticed only from his voice that he had been crying. He could no longer pull his hands out of the handcuffs. 'Make your hands small,' commanded our comrade teacher but no one knew quite how that was supposed to work.

She let out a sigh and said, 'Children, children—why can't you just behave?'

Then she took off the bunches of bracelets she always wore, which clattered when she wrote on the blackboard and conducted chorus, so that all the 'big kids' said, 'Man oh man, we'd have loved to be lucky enough to have such a modern comrade.' Ileana was allowed to hold all the bracelets and she was bursting with pride.

'Come on,' said our comrade teacher, and began pulling on Virgil's arms with all her might. 'Make one peep and you'll regret it,' she added for good measure, but his little hands didn't come out, not even when she spat on his wrists to make the handcuffs slide more easily.

'Do you want to rest for a minute, and we'll take over for you?' Ileana asked in her sing-songy voice, but our comrade teacher paid no attention because she was busy rolling up Virgil's sleeves so they wouldn't get bloodied. His wrists were badly abraded.

'And now they're swelling up, too,' said our comrade teacher. When she thought she heard a giggle, she shot back at us, 'You little shitheads.' She was on the brink of tears, 'Unworthy! You're all totally unworthy of the red tie!'

She asked for a clean handkerchief.

'Grab my bag,' she told Ileana, whose stiff arms were straight out and still holding the many bracelets in her hands, but I had already pulled my bag over. 'Here, take my handkerchief, the edges smell of cologne but it's clean.' Our comrade teacher then rolled it up and ordered Virgil to bite down on it as hard as he could, so he wouldn't feel the pain as much. 'As hard as you can,' repeated Ileana, ostensibly out of concern for Virgil.

And then our comrade teacher grabbed Virgil's arms, pulled and pulled, and his eyes nearly popped right out of their sockets. 'You're almost there,' said Ileana, and our comrade teacher propped herself against the wall behind Virgil with both legs, yanking harder. When even that didn't work, she gave up and let Virgil—whose arms appeared as if they'd grown out of the same wall they now looked nailed to—slump into a heap on the floor. And then she took it out on us, 'Miserable miscreants, go to hell, just hang yourselves with your shitty red ties, why don't you? Shitty children! Shitty little shits! This shit sucks!'

After this fit she quickly regained her composure, rummaged through her bag and pulled out a little blue container labelled 'Nivea'.

'What's that?' Ileana asked in her sing-songy voice.

'A medicinal cream,' said our comrade teacher, 'can't you see he's bleeding?'

She spread the cream on Virgil's hands and wrists, and with all her strength tried yet again to pull him out of the handcuffs. When that didn't work, she held on to his limp body and lifted her legs off the floor. A few years ago, I saw a shaky film clip of a woman in Iraq who did the same thing with a hanged man so he would die faster and suffer less.

Virgil wasn't moving, but couldn't be freed from the handcuffs either, so our comrade teacher put all her bracelets on again and led us back. 'Sing as loud as you can,' she commanded us, in case Virgil happened to wake up and start screaming. We left him there like that, my handkerchief still in his mouth.

I sang loudly not because I wanted to follow orders but because I was intent on outsinging the overbearing Ileana. And so I was selected—the comrade inspector came to me after the ceremony in which we all got our red ties and said, 'Have you ever dreamt of giving flowers to our supreme comrades?' Whereupon our comrade teacher burst into tears and hugged me.

Then she invited all the other children to hug me, first Ileana, commandant of our troop division, who was quite confused by this unexpected outcome, and then the girl who was commandant of the window row, because I sat in the row of desks closest to the window at school, and then the other commandants, too, of the door row and the two middle rows. The comrade inspector laughed and said, 'Are there only girl commandants in your class?' Our comrade teacher cheerfully replied that the top students were always girls, and then the comrade inspector said something like, 'Girls are always the best, even later.' She laughed the entire bus trip back to Bucharest, and because the comrade inspector accompanied us, we couldn't go back to get Virgil.

I can't quite remember exactly how the rest of it went, or I've forgotten the order of events at least, but I do know that first of all my parents congratulated me and then, when we were on an afternoon walk and I noticed there was no one in sight, I asked them to tell me the truth. 'Which truth?' 'You don't like him.' My mother looked at me, horrified, 'You mean our supreme comrade?' And then she slapped me, 'How could you say such a stupid thing?' and ran home howling.

Only later did I learn that my parents had separated for a bit, for that very reason. I had been sent away for a while, to undergo some medical examinations, so I hadn't known at the time. But I met a bunch of nice nurses who were convinced I would become a radio star on the show *Sing Song Minisong*, and travel to Budapest and Prague, and maybe even the GDR. And another comrade class-leader lady also visited me a lot, bringing me sweets and telling me about Mother—that is, our supreme mother, mother of all the people, who liked being addressed as 'Mother'. 'Don't worry, she's very kind, just like a normal mother, even better.' This mother's picture hung in my room, she was young and beautiful as a fairy, with lovely hair and big, bright eyes.

And then came the big day. I got a huge bouquet of red roses or tulips but I've forgotten everything, all the children who were there, all the songs we sang, and whether I opened my mouth to sing at all or just moved my lips like I did at school, simply because it amused Mémé when I told her about it afterward. 'Mémé, last year I even imitated animal sounds during the anthem. The blonde girl, Ileana, told on me, but our comrade teacher asked me if it was so, and I said no.' Mémé laughed and said, 'Oh, that must've driven Ileana mad.'

But the reality was different, I had received a royal walloping from the entire class. Our comrade teacher had held me and walked me past every fellow student, and all my comrade classmates were allowed to hit me as hard as they could. On that day all my friendships ended, even my friendship with little Virgil who continued protesting that he had only made it look as if he had hit me, and not even with all his strength. 'I'll bet you want to see what it's like when I hit you as hard as I can, huh?' he threatened, as I 'continued acting' as if I were offended, or so he claimed.

But now I was the one who was allowed to meet the supreme comrades, and I climbed the stairs to steady applause, clap-clap-clap, clap-clap-clap. The sound propelled me forward like a strong wind at my back, I teared up, and everyone I passed gave me a pat on the shoulder. 'Bravo, child,' 'Bravo' and 'Bravo, you are the future.' And then the voices of a children's choir rose from somewhere, singing 'When we're no longer children, we'll all lend a hand'. A sea of colourful flags fluttered over the whole scene, like millions of colourful birds, before unexpectedly freezing in front of the blood-red carpet, forming the exact shape of my bouquet.

Then there was a long silence, no motion whatsoever as far as the eye could see. It was as if I were suddenly all alone, and all the people around me were dolls.

'Is this bouquet for me?' asked an old woman with a potato nose.

'No,' I said.

'For whom is it, then?'

Out of the corner of my eye I looked towards the comrade class-leader lady who gazed into the distance with unbridled joy.

'It is for me,' said the old woman with the potato nose.

'It's not for you, because it's for my mother!'

'For your mother?' the old woman asked with an evil grin, 'And where is your mother?'

I looked around but everything was frozen stiff.

'She's coming,' I said, to stall the old woman until help came.

But the old woman had already grabbed the bunch of flowers and was trying to pull it from my hands. I held on with all my strength. And then came the deafening noise, the applause, and thousands of comrades chanted and waved huge pictures of our dear Mother overhead as she briefly continued to stare at me.

I stayed on the grandstand all afternoon, since the comrade class-leader lady had begged me to stay by the old woman with the potato nose. 'Look what lovely braids you have, and such big pom-pom hair ties,' she said to me, 'have you ever seen such big pom-poms? And you know what? We'll wait until the end, and then we'll ask if you can take the pom-poms home with you.' So apparently I stayed there, shaking my head the entire time so that my braids waved, and they even saw me on TV. By then my mother had already returned home, and my parents watched the whole thing on Rapineau's TV, with its three-colour layer of film, alongside a bunch of friends and neighbours. 'What colour was my bouquet?' I asked. My father laughed with pride, and said, 'Blue.'

22

As I come to the table the men look at me inquisitively, or at least they quickly turn their classic Ray-Ban Cats sunglasses towards me. I take a seat on one of the rattan chairs and ask the waitress to bring something to drink.

'She even reads books about architecture,' Flavian says softly to his friend.

The waitress brings an empty glass and pours me a bit from the bottle she then puts back into a cooler on our table.

'Elit by Stolichnaya—The Himalayan Edition,' Flavian says cheerfully, and the spot of sun glinting from one of his lenses makes him look a little clownish. 'Be sure to sip it very slowly, darling.'

'No worries,' says his friend, 'we can always just order another bottle, no problem.'

'No, the only problem is that he's trying to bribe me,' Flavian says to me.

The two burst into laughter, figuring it will cover up the embarrassment of having been overheard during a private conversation. The terrace turns like a carousel but it can't be because of the vodka yet. And music starts up again, or has merely changed, overlapping itself, the different beats piling atop one another.

'This is fantastic,' says the little Indian, 'just like in Greece.'

'*Ela re malaka*, next time take us with you,' says Flavian.

'I'll take you along, bitch,' says the little Indian, 'I'll bring all my bitches, so it'll be more fun.'

Their laughter has real rhythm, even during the pauses, and were it not for the background music it would put me right to sleep. 'Black Hair, Lily-Filled Air' comes on, 'In celebration of Carol Felix's centenary,' the radio DJ announces, and I down my entire glass.

Did I actually tell Flavian that my great-grandparents' house supposedly stood right here on Arsenal Hill? When Mémé jumped out the window one starlit night to run off with Carol Felix—who at the time was a chansonnier and diseur famous only in Bucharest—she wore only her nightie and took nothing but her hairbrush.

She had gorgeous, curly hair that was pitch-black her entire life. It was probably just good genes but she attributed it to the fact that she brushed it three times a day, carefully counting one hundred strokes each time—sometimes she'd brush it a bit more, to make up for the days when her arms hurt, but her arms never hurt, not even at the very end. Carol Felix wrote his famous love song 'Black Hair, Lily-Filled Air' for her, and shortly thereafter he became a celebrity with 'You Stick to My Soul Like the Stamp on a Love Letter'.

When Mémé left him, he stopped writing his own songs, but his success didn't suffer—quite the contrary, his versions of songs by Yves Montand and a few Italian songwriters took off, and his interpretation of Bixio's 'Vivere' gained worldwide fame. Flavian sings along:

Oggi che magnifica giornata,
Che giornata di felicità
La mia bella donna se n'è andata M'ha lasciato
alfine in libertà
...
Ella m'ha giurato nel partir
Che non sarebbe ritornata mai più

The little Indian grins, 'Nice, nice!'

The waitress has lowered the music inside, and now stands by our table, laughing. And we continue, with the refrain:

Ridere sempre così giocondo
Ridere delle follie del mondo
Vivere finché c'è gioventù
Perché la vita e bella
La voglio vivere sempre più

The little Indian enthusiastically applauds, and I can almost see the old Carol Felix in front of me, his hair dyed yet still stylishly tousled, his jacket covered in badges. There was one, of course, that read 'Fighter'—the moniker anticommunist protesters were initially insulted by, until they claimed it as a badge of honour. But there was also one with the royal coat of arms as well as ones you can get in church right next to the candles, portraying archangels Michael and Gabriel as well as Bucharest's patron, St Demetrius of Basarabov. And he always had a blue hibiscus blossom on the back of his jacket, exactly like the ones that grew near the National Theatre.

'Let's go by and see what's going on,' my mother would say as she came home from work. She wouldn't even change her clothes, just her shoes if they'd been splattered by the goop used for fillings. 'Please, Dimi, make sure you get them clean, otherwise I could cry.' But luckily she found an elegant pair to wear to the demonstrations, and then she just had to freshen up her make-up and spritz a bit of perfume on the ball of her thumbs and behind her ear lobes. 'All right, then, hurry up.'

As soon as we got there we went straight to Carol Felix, to say hello. I think the very first time I met him was there. 'He's holding down the fort,' my mother and father both said in alternation. 'We can count on him.' He could always be found to the left of the fountain, near the architectural school, by the candelabra—one was lit for the living, the other for the martyrs.

'But how could they have been martyrs if there wasn't any revolution?' I asked my father.

Then my father explained that, at the time, people had thought it was indeed a revolution. They had sacrificed themselves in this belief, and in the end their faith was all that counted—their firm faith, for which they had sacrificed everything—coup d'état or not. And as my father made these statements, people gathered round to join the discussion. They were friendly people, men with beards and moustaches and friendly smiles, constantly puffing smoke, and well-dressed women who smelt of perfume and the peroxide from their perms. They agreed it was up to us to ensure that these people hadn't died in vain, and we could do so by making our own lives meaningful. Divinity lay in sacrifice, in the kind of noble generosity Christ had modelled for us—the willingness to give everything, at any time, even life itself, so that the twists and turns and clashes of history could find resolution and the whole of existence find its flow.

By candlelight Carol Felix told us what had happened that day and whom he had met. Theatre actors, singers, professors, priests, intellectuals—but also simple people, with big hearts. 'A big heart, Victoria, let me tell you, a big heart lets you open your eyes and broaden your mind. Nihil sine Deo, Victoria, that's what it says on the royal Romanian coat of arms: nothing without God!'

He asked about Mémé. 'One ought stick together at such times,' he said, but Mémé continued protesting in her usual spot, the meeting point near the clock, so she could make a quick getaway to the bus station without crowds. She was always with two childhood friends she'd met at the Sisters of Loreto boarding school. One invariably had perfect nail polish without the slightest scratch while the other always had chipped nail polish. It's not that she did more manual work than her friend, she was just a bit sloppier, although only when it came to her manicure. On University Square I saw these two life-long friends of Mémé for the first and last time but I didn't know who was who because I didn't dare look at their nails.

I ran into my housekeeper there, too. Mrs Jeny was with her four or five grandchildren who were all wearing my hand-me-downs and knelt for both the national anthem as well as the 'Fighters' Anthem'.

'Let's at least stay until the fighters' anthem,' Mrs Jeny encouraged the children when they started complaining and wanted to go home, and it sounded as if they were in church and she was telling them, 'Let's at least stay until the Our Father.'

And as much as they complained they were thirsty or were getting sunstroke or had to go to the toilet, those kids had a sure sense of when the long-awaited fighters' anthem was going to start because they knelt as if on cue. Like churchgoers who kneel before reciting the Our Father, they either knew the liturgy or just sensed when it was time for intercessions and all the rest:

Better hobo
than traitor!
Better roughneck
than dictator!
Better fighter
than activist!
Better DEAD
than communist!

The kneeling children were soon joined by nuns and students, all of whom knelt on the left side of the street in front of the National Theatre, where a monument was later erected with towering boundary markers declaring the spot 'Ground Zero of Democracy'.

Except for those who were kneeling, everyone jumped as they sang, raising their arms and moving their hands in a pulsating, rhythmic crescendo, culminating in the shouted-out 'better DEAD!' The fathers, especially, belted it out frightfully, almost louder than even Carol Felix. 'Better DEAD,' as if it were a threat to someone who would regret being dead. Fathers opened up. Sometimes fathers and sons hugged each other during the anthem, and the force of one's shouts drew the other's.

In the days following, one of the speakers on a university-building balcony started the refrain, 'Better hobo . . . ,' and the crowd added, 'than traitor . . . than dictator . . . than activist', but they never let loose the ultimate shout, the shout to drown out all others, 'Better DEAD.' And it sounded like a jubilation, a joke much more indecorous than the ones I used to tell, 'Better DEAD.'

At the time I also met many people who were relatives, distant relatives or close family friends, but after the demonstrations were crushed I never saw them again. It's not that they died during the Mineriads when armed miners came from the north to violently confront the protesters. I don't think any of them have even died.

Carol Felix stayed a hundred yards from his beloved Mémé, at the fountain, because he lived just around the corner on Academy Street, opposite St Nicholas Russian Church. He hadn't seen Mémé since they split after the war. 'Why did you break up?' I had once asked Mémé, but she didn't really know. 'It was just the times we were living in,' she said.

'Have they taught you what class struggle is in school?' Carol Felix asked me every time. I always said no, because I knew he liked to tell me. 'Class struggle is the struggle between people with fewer school classes against those with more classes—or at least with more class!'

We'd laugh long and hard, and then look up at the university-building balcony because we didn't know what else to say. I remember his loud voice so well. 'Down with the communists,' he shouted, as if I weren't standing right next to him. He'd get everyone else going, too, and a thunderous response from University Square followed—thousands of Bucharesters' voices rang out, all the way to the Intercontinental Hotel, the National Theatre and then across the road to Queen Elisabeth Boulevard.

Carol Felix invited me over once, just once, when a concert of the three tenors was being broadcast, so he decided not to go to the demonstrations. 'We can watch it together,' he said. I still remember my shadow on Academy Street, nobody else was out walking and my shadow grew longer and longer. In one hand I carried a package from Confiserie Capsa, in the other a bouquet of lilies. Just as I passed St Nicholas Russian Church a plastic bag full of urine fell on my head from the third floor of building 23, and I heard someone yell 'Fascists!' from above. Looking up I saw the shadow of a retreating figure.

Although this happened on a street parallel to University Square, where the chants of a loud chorus were starting, there wasn't a soul in sight until I reached the architecture school. I spent the evening hiding in the architecture school toilets, and only went home after my parents were fast asleep.

After that intense period of anticommunist demonstrations, I never saw Carol Felix again. 'He's just a very private person,' my father said.

He recorded his last album at eighty-four, *Carol Felix's Favourite Tunes*. It apparently became one of the best-selling Romanian records of all time. In the end, the old master had wanted to include one or two anti-communist protest songs but the Electrecord studio supposedly had a problem securing the rights. I have a hard time imagining it but the composer of almost all those protest songs recently died of tuberculosis. He was barely fifty years old, dirt poor and completely forgotten, living in obscurity in a small flat near University Square. Shortly before his death he had been awarded the 'Revolutionary Certificate' for his contribution to the cause. He would never have accepted it but a poet friend of his did her best to interpret what he'd have wanted had he not needed the money so badly.

One thing I cannot remember at all is Carol Felix's funeral—I can't even say exactly where he's buried, because I had since hired a plot caretaker and started paying her a monthly salary to tend all our family graves. It may well be that he's buried in the same crypt as Mémé's favourite uncle Neagu.

'Don't you worry, Madame Director,' the chief security officer of the security firm from my bank assured me. I hired them to put an end to the disgrace that had befallen our fine family tomb. For decades now the crypt's northern wall had been lined with the stubs of burnt-out candles which suggests someone goes there to perform some ritual curse. Word has it an unbelievably old woman sneaks in and out at night, a hunchback who's shrunk to the size of a child, and stands only half as tall as the statue of women in mourning by Raffaelo Romanelli which are clothed only by their long hair. I wonder whether she's come back again and the 'Chief', as we call him at work, lets her keep doing her thing while holding out on me.

'Could be,' says Flavian, promising to take care of it.

'Maybe you just have to ask the plot caretaker to keep an eye on the Chief,' says the little Indian.

And then he tells us about his own grandmother who is now also buried in Bellu cemetery in a beautiful crypt with wall paintings by Constantin Lecca, right near his other grandmother. But the other had died before he was born, so this was the only one he got to know. 'She was a huge Carol Felix fan, and was also the first Miss Romania, I swear.' He has pictures of her wearing the Miss-Romania tiara and a velvet cloak that was far too long for her. But he only knew her as the elderly resident of a one-bedroom flat in Ferentari, one of Bucharest's most derelict neighbourhoods. How she ended up there was a long story even she herself had forgotten. And she wouldn't accept any help, he says, she didn't want any handouts—no gifts, no radio, no TV, no chair. Her only furniture was a worn-out sofa bed and a table. Once the little Indian had given her a pair of drinking glasses, and she had thrown one away. 'I only need one,' she said, 'there's only one of me.'

Flavian wants to know whether she was still beautiful in her old age. The little Indian says he's unfit to judge—after all, she was his grandmother.

'But yeah, sure, as beautiful as I am,' he then says, and the two burst into fraternal laughter yet again. I'm waiting for one of the guys, or at least the little Indian, to ask where the young Ms Née-Moinescu is but neither of them ask. They just sit there telling one story after another. Each seems sadder than the next, but it's also true that one sadness can lighten yet another sadness, or at least offset it. Because that's life, right? You have to take it as it comes. And they don't ask after Victoria even when the waitress clears away the fourth glass at our table.

So on to the next story. The little Indian didn't have a computer at home but already sensed he was good with them. His school had a computer lab with five computers, but it was always full, there was never a single computer station free. What did he do, then? When the power went out one day and the computer lab was empty, he crept over to one of the computers and wiped the letters off the keys using his mother's nail-polish remover. He knew the entire keyboard by heart, every letter and every number, so from then on it basically became his personal computer. Bravo, *re malaka*, even as a child you were a criminal.

Flavian and I toast and drink to him, the little Indian toasts and drinks to himself and then we all look at each other and throw our glasses high over the parapet in a synchronized pitch. 'Just like in Greece, *malaka*, like in Greece!'

The waitress takes a pile of money from the little Indian and walks off with a spring in her step, then turns the music up even louder. It's an entirely different genre now, some kind of gangsta rap. The little Indian says goodbye, it seems he'd almost forgotten a business meeting. '*Malaka, malaka*,' he says to his old friend Flavian, patting him on the head. 'When I'm back from San Francisco we'll all go to the Mediterranean!' He gallantly kisses my hand, then takes off.

And I suppose he plans to meet his wife 'in the People's House', or maybe not. But I don't get a chance to tell Flavian that she's fallen from the balcony because he's busy proposing to me.

23

Codrin's office is on the eighth and top floor of the Opera Centre, a hulking block of bluish glass and brown marble. This last touch seems to have been inspired by the colour and shape of the little old brick building catercorner which was a public toilet before being renovated as the Rio Bar. The window offers a blue-tinted view of the square I used to cross on foot, by bus or by tram every single day of my now distant-seeming past—it feels so far back I'd almost say it was in my 'previous life'. When I was afraid of being caught riding without a ticket, I'd spring for a car service or taxi. I crossed it both alone and in company, exhilarated and depressed, in sandals, platforms, sneakers and boots. I even crossed it barefoot once, after going to the opera with Dinu, when we got caught in a sudden downpour. I stomped rhythmically through the puddles, as if dancing the Habanera, until the cracking voice of the transvestite reached me through the curtains of rain,

'Like peasants, my God, just like peasants!' I can still see the transvestite crouched before me on his wooden crate, his posture perfect, a small umbrella in his left hand, constantly fanning himself with his right hand. 'Fresh air, my God, I need some fresh air.' His hands are petite and delicate, like the leaf of an ornamental plant—like a red-leaf Japanese maple, as I later discovered in Zurich's Bäckeranlage park, where a lot of people walk around barefoot.

And he's still there now, my old acquaintance, wearing an airy summer dress and oversized straw hat that's constantly on the verge of being blown off. With the hand that isn't holding the hat he's waving at the cars driving by. It's the kind of wave you'd see on the French Riviera, or in a movie filmed there. There's the same shimmering light that blurs the edges of everything, and a few cars always stop but just briefly—ever since I was a kid, I remember cars always stopping there, only to speed off again, their tires screeching.

The streetlights are still on, yellow points of light on an already dazzling summer morning. Small flags from a recent national holiday still hang from the lampposts. The Dambovita's water sparkles and a small boy, perhaps Arnold, sits on the bridge feeding pigeons in the shadow of the yellow sign with the smiley face that reads, 'You are leaving the Cotroceni district.'

Farther to the left, at the start of Dr Joseph Lister Street, the most spectacular accidents occur despite the relative lack of traffic. This is where cars from St Eleutherius Street, Heroes' Boulevard and Independence Road turn at full speed, disregarding others' right of way because most of the drivers are busy crossing themselves, as people do in front of every church. The accident-prone spot is also right where the street artist Kelemen has painted a zebra with red and white stripes. The red paint has worn off a bit, and from up here the zebra looks surprisingly three-dimensional, like an animal resting on its side, breathing imperceptibly.

Every time I see the jagged signature 'Kelemen' scrawled somewhere in the city, I wonder if this Kelemen is my former lover who lived near here, in the house that's now a restaurant called Museum. He had a tabby cat, neutered, so it wouldn't chase birds. 'Neutered cats don't hunt birds,' Kelemen had told me. I still remember exactly where he said this—it was on the stairs to his attic, and his face was red from the sun. 'Neutered cats don't hunt birds' hardly seems like anything he would ever say, but it's the only thing he said that I still remember. It's also untrue.

'Nice animal,' I say, and Codrin nods beside me.

'Zebra', by the way, was also the right answer to the only radio contest I ever participated in and won. I had wanted to tape a song with my cassette recorder, and was holding the microphone a few centimetres from the speaker when the radio DJ started talking over the last few bars of music. 'Today's riddle is—horse in pyjamas!'

I grabbed the phone and my call went right through. Instead of cursing, as I had planned, I blurted out, 'Zebra! The answer is zebra!' The DJ rejoiced, 'Hurraaah, we have a winner!' And then I said that 'horse in a prison uniform' would've been a more fitting clue than 'horse in pyjamas'.

Codrin laughs and says, 'Let's leave the horse in pyjamas!'

As I take a seat on the leather chair a cold breeze with a whiff of citronella inadvertently makes me assume the stiffly professional demeanour I usually have when working at the bank. Codrin's automatic way of offering me coffee and asking 'sugar or sweetener?' and finally 'surely you'll have a cookie?' suggests he interprets my restraint as a sort of shyness or admiration, so he loosens his tie, slides back in his chair, tucks his hands behind his head, exposing his golden cufflinks and confesses that this legal practice actually belongs to a distant uncle, but he almost never comes into the office and plans to leave everything to him.

'Caesar,' I say, and although I no longer remember why I used to call Codrin Caesar, I suddenly see he dislikes the nickname just as much now as he did way back when. 'Caesar,' I say with a more conciliatory tone, 'I'm not here because of your communist uncle, you know that. I'm here despite all that, because we know and trust each other.'

As I'm saying this, a very young employee comes in with some papers to be signed and then leaves again, her face crimson red. Codrin pushes a button to summon her back, signs the papers and watches her as she walks back out. It seems to me he's looking at her behind.

'We can take the case,' he says, and stands up. 'Don't worry. You just had some bad luck.'

I follow his example and stand.

'It's not a matter of bad luck.'

We look at each other, and Codrin laughs the engaging laugh of a winning lawyer.

'Call it what you will, but let it be our business, no one else's.'

24

I cannot vouch that this story is completely true, not because I forgot how it went but, rather, because I couldn't read it clearly. I can remember the circumstances, though—exactly when and where I caught sight of this book of illustrated anecdotes. Little Codrin was sitting on the stairs outside the front door, bent over the text, and was probably just waiting for me to ask him what he was doing and whether I could read along. I read over his shoulder but stayed standing, so I had a perfect view of the drawing to the left of the text depicting two old men in a swimming pool. I've had to fill in the blanks here and there, but the story goes something like this:

An ascetic visits a filthy rich man in his palace, eats and drinks a sumptuous feast with him, tours the verdant gardens and then joins him in the sauna. 'How can you live like this?' asks the ascetic, as they sit facing each other naked. 'All this wealth is a mirage, it keeps you from seeing what's truly important. You have everything, but you are bound to it like a millstone. Ye cannot serve God and Mammon. As you know, it is easier for a camel to go through the eye of a needle than for a rich man to enter into the kingdom of God. Those who hang onto earthly riches will not find salvation.' The rich man listens to his guest, sweats and grows more and more anxious. But then, unforeseeably, a terrible fire breaks out in the palace, and within no time all the rich man's possessions have gone up in the blaze. The two men manage to save themselves only by jumping into the pool, still naked. And while the formerly rich host floats on his back in the water and watches everything he owned burn to the ground, the ascetic starts making his way out of the pool. 'God, oh God, I've left my ascetic's robe in there.'

'It's too dangerous to go back in,' his host warns. 'It could be fatal.'

'But that's my only worldly possession,' cries the ascetic, jumping into the fire.

I have often asked myself exactly how rich is rich enough—at what point will I feel set enough to just calmly watch everything burn to the ground and maintain my composure. I've actually always felt that my destiny would lead me towards just such a purifying fire, putting me to the ultimate test, whereupon I'd achieve complete spiritual freedom. As a result, I had interpreted countless small occurrences as the larger, longed-for turning point, and had acted accordingly—that is, from anyone else's perspective, with no plan whatsoever. Or, to use my mother's words, 'like a leaf on a breeze'.

On this particular late afternoon it seems some sort of end is nigh because, while my parents perform their obligatory holiday visits with old friends, Flavian is going to pick up his ladies and their priest friend, and Mrs Jeny is in the kitchen putting the last touches on the meal, bustling about and smiling when I remark that the vegetable milk soup is the most important dish. As all that is going on, the doorbell rings and I open it to find a man in sweaty pancake make-up who greets me with an old-fashioned air of reverence.

Looking up again after a chivalrous bow, he takes two steps back and declares as if he were onstage, with enough volume and enunciation for it to echo through the entire stairwell, 'Victoria, my Victoria, let me admire you—you've stolen my heart and soul, and look more enchanting than ever.'

I push the guest back out and the door clacks shut with a sound harsh enough to reverberate through my neighbour Dobrescu's palatial flat.

'Try again.'

The man in make-up takes a deep, triple bow, pressing his palms together, after which he smoothes his crumpled, blood-stained shirt and starts reciting:

O come, my treasure fair and far
And thy world leave aside;
I am the light, bright evening star
And thou shalt be my bride.

I ponder whether this is the right time to kiss him, although he's still made-up. I probably take a little too much time thinking it over, because Dobrescu, irritated by the silence, calls up the stairs, 'Was it your doorbell they rang, Miss Victoria?'

'Yes, it was mine,' I say.

'So it was, all right then.'

Speaking in a hushed voice, the uninvited guest says he simply had to come over as soon as he heard about it. He was in Herastrau Park when he got word of it, so he went out and took the first bus, route 331. In Floreasca he saw a pretzel vendor and whistled over to him—I wonder how long he must've kept the bus door blocked, and then realize just as long as it took him to say 'the big one with pumpkin seeds'—and the vendor ran over to put all his remaining pretzels on the guy's arm. Then a guy with a bandaged head came up and said, 'You want us all to look like fools, or what?'

We're seated in the side yard, in the garden under the grape arbour, and the guest goes on and on. He talks louder and louder, his fork hovering over the apricot crepe as if any moment now he were about to take a bite.

'You want us all to look like fools, or what?' he says, 'Yeah, I want you all to look like fools, you got a problem with that?' The guy looks at him with one eye, the other is under the bandage, then without a word he goes towards the front of the bus and takes a seat.

Ticket-checkers get on, a shiver of anxious excitement becomes palpable in the air, then they get off again near the British Council Centre in Dorobanti.

By the time he gets off the bus at Roman Square, he's long since forgotten the guy with the bandaged head, but then he reappears, coming at him with five other guys who are all pounding their fists into their palms. He punches one of them out to defend his honour but then the rest of them give him a pummelling until his bus comes, so it was quite a beating.

'And you know what I thought of as I lay on the ground, Victoria? I thought of you, because I thought it would soon be over—I though it was the end.'

In the flower shop next to the colonnade, the place that now sells mobile phones but which everyone still calls 'the flower shop', a salesman helps him clean up a bit and gives him a clean shirt with a mobile phone on it. But it doesn't go with his make-up, or what's left of it, at least. He also doesn't want to change his shirt in front of anyone because of the faux tattoo the make-up artists painted while he was on set—he still has a shred of decency—so he decides to just leave it be.

He goes back to the bus stop but nothing comes for what feels like forever, so he goes to the next stop, and then the next stop, near the evangelical church, where a taxi driver looks him up and down and tosses him an insult. 'What's up with you, faggot, can't you afford a taxi?' He walks straight through Cismigiu Park where it's shady and quiet. The only people there are old men just sitting around a bunch of pansy-beds and staring at each other or off into space, it's utterly dismal. 'I wanted to play chess,' he overhears someone saying as he walks by, 'but it reeks of urine near the chess tables, and there's nobody there, either.' By then he's as far as the Boulevard, by the Cervantes stop, or whatever that bus stop by the newly renovated Hotel Cismigiu is called. For some reason he asks if it reminds me of that song, 'Welcome to the Hotel Cismigiu—such a lovely place, such a lovely place, such a lovely face . . . ?'

And the bus he finally boards is almost empty, so that he immediately spots them—the men from before!

He looks at them and can't believe his eyes. He starts laughing, and the men look at him as he doubles over with laughter at the back of the bus. They laugh, too, and point at one another and laugh—he at the men and the men at him. 'Unbelievable,' they say with a sing-songy Moldovian accent. 'It's unbelievable.' One of them pulls out a tissue and wipes his tears, then everyone wants a tissue and then finally they offer him one. They get off before the opera but before leaving they ask him directions—they'd like to go to the palm house. There are some palm trees in Odessa, too, but who wants to go all the way to Odessa nowadays, to fucking Russia, and then back home?

'Is there anything like that in the Botanical Garden, Victoria, or did I give them the wrong directions?'

'Every major nightclub has palm trees at the entrance,' I told him.

'Those are Ficus trees, Victoria!'

'Palms!'

'Ficus!'

I point to the crepes and recommend he eat them, since I don't have all day.

He'll eat them later, he says—first he'd like to address the reason he looks the way he does. He asks if I recognize who he's made-up to look like.

I don't.

I shouldn't act like that, he says, otherwise he'll take off his T-shirt, and Dobrescu can watch us from the balcony.

'Go ahead,' I say.

But then he starts eating the crepes.

Maybe an opera character? I'd have to think about which genre, perhaps Rigoletto or Peter Grimes? Faust? Or no, wait, he's Herman from *The Queen of Spades*!

'Tri karty, tri karty, tri karty . . .' he sings, reciting the 'Three cards' aria, his mouth full. 'Obsessiveness suits me, don't you think?'

His character wasn't from an opera, although now that I've said that, he wonders what he might have missed out on. No, his character was from a film, and he had now been given the role of the legendary Captain Botev—the whole role, not just the stunts.

I congratulate him, and then he enthusiastically tells me how it happened that they chose him, the stuntman, for the entire part. This was, after all, a long and complex story with many main characters and a lot of romantic intrigue—a Romanian-French co-production shot in the port cities of Tulcea, Istanbul and Marseille. I peek at my watch. I shouldn't act like that, he says, especially because the whole reason he's come out here is so I'll be the first to know. Did Mémé ever tell me about Botev? No. He doesn't want to disappoint, quite the contrary, he aims to surprise and inspire, so he figures the best way to prepare would be to see how Botev's widow reacts to his acting, and maybe even ask her some questions about the young captain. It's essential that he know how to reincarnate the historical figure to a certain degree, like performing a re-enactment—not that that's what the director expects of him but, rather, because he himself needs it in order to play the part more convincingly. He goes on and on about himself and Marseilles and the delicious bouillabaisse he ate on the right side of the harbour, Chez Aldo, where the rattling of the ships' masts reminded him of our streets back in Cotroceni. Did I still remember the light clinking sound those milk bottles made? 'Want to come with me to Marseilles?'

'Sure,' I say as I stand up. 'Why not?'

But he yanks the plate from my hand, saying I can't just throw him out when there's still so much left unsaid. If he needs therapy he should go see his mother, I tell him. He laughs, and I laugh and I sit down. And so the time passes, perhaps we talk a bit. But in any case, I don't get the chance to fetch another portion of crepes, as I'd meant to—I keep saying I'll stay for one more sentence, and then I'll come back with a fresh plate of crepes, but I never even get up. The dried-out, dangling linden blossoms start to rustle, like a muffled drum roll playing with our expectations.

And then Flavian comes back with Sorana and Mami Cordelia and their friend the priest, and they all stay in the side yard under the grape arbour with Dinu whom I've just introduced them to and to whom the ladies take an immediate liking. 'Might you have a cigarette for Mami? No? Great, that's even better, this way she won't smoke.' The priest sits there too, at the head of the table, with a kindly smile. Flavian discreetly asks me whether he should get a clean shirt for our guest. I nod, and we go upstairs together, but then Mrs Jeny interrupts us and we forget the shirt. 'Once you're back downstairs, we'll set the table there,' she says, bustling up and down the stairs a few times with empty trays, pots and bottles. Every step of the way she makes a 'sssss' sound, just like when she's ironing, which makes the gathering sound even busier. Then everyone eats and drinks and talks, all in a hurry, as if everyone had to leave again, but then came one more glass, naturally, and stuffed peppers, and again one last little glass, and then crème brulée, of course, but only a small portion, and then the obligatory, 'Mrs Jeny, come sit with us,' and her even more obligatory, 'Later.' Another time she declines by saying, 'I was eating the entire time I was cooking, I can't even look at food any more,' but she says she'll stay for the toast. The priest says, 'To Victoria and Flavian,' lifting the glass as if he were lifting the holy chalice.

'To us all,' I say, peering from the corner of my eyes at Dinu who has leant back far enough to disappear behind Sorana. We drink, Mrs Jeny drinks with us, and then Flavian tells everyone about my vineyards which aren't quite mine because the son of the mayor from the neighbouring village got them. 'They're all criminals,' says Sorana. But a vineyard of the same size had finally been returned to me, Flavian continued, and it was the same as it always had been—same grapevines, of the same age, on a slope with the same inclination and the same exposure, very sunny—only the posts and wires were missing because gypsies had stolen them years ago for scrap metal. 'There are criminals everywhere,' says Sorana, it's a shame the vines are growing on the ground now, downslope. 'Don't you like the wine?' her son asks. 'Sure,' she says, but it's sad to see a vineyard with all its vines on the ground, growing between weeds. 'But who would replace the posts, Mother, we don't know what's involved, and the farmer says the vines are too old anyway, and should be torn out.' 'Yes, everything old should be torn out,' says Sorana, getting worked up by the wine. 'There isn't any other farmer nearby who could do it,' the priest interjects, as if he knew all about it, and we all nod—who would dare take on the local gypsies out there? 'They're all criminals!' And then Mami Cordelia stirs—because she hadn't been smoking, she'd noticeably drooped a bit and looked somewhat absent, as if a cigarette would've been a worthy occupation, the glowing butt between her fingers energizing her hand enough to set the rhythm for her next hoarsely whispered statement—and turns to Dinu.

'Are you the grandson of Miclescu—Colonel Miclescu?'

Now all eyes are on Dinu. He sits up straight and begins to tell another of his long tales, about his grandfather, the venerable Colonel. He had never actually met him, of course, but everyone who had known him would say his grandson, meaning Dinu, looked a lot like him—Mami Cordelia nods—a whole lot like him. Indeed, they resembled each other so much that, looking at old photos, one could easily confuse the two. The colonel had been arrogant and brutal, according to his contemporaries, but also constantly surrounded by women. 'Which you surely are, as well,' says Sorana.

But here's what happened to Colonel Miclescu—he went out one evening with a lady. 'With Piggy Lahovary,' says Mami Cordelia in her painfully scratchy voice, and Sorana adds, 'A high-society lady from a political family, as in the three foreign ministers Iacob, Ioan and Alexandru Lahovary.' Not to mention that Colonel Miclescu was a 'vieux marcheur' who took her from club to club, from the Corso to the chic lounges on Victory Road, and then they went dancing at the place across from the former Hotel Louvre—supposedly they were already drunk when they got there. Young Carol Felix was there, singing his love songs 'Black Hair, Lily-Filled Air' and 'You Stick to My Soul Like the Stamp on a Love Letter', and Colonel Miclescu and Piggy danced, tightly entwined. After that no one knows precisely what happened because Claymoor, the omnipresent gossip columnist, apparently came down with a migraine and left astonishingly early. He had been there when the two of them arrived, and wanted to keep a close eye out for what he liked to call 'les faits du cancan', the juicy grist for his popular column 'Carnet du High-Life' in *L'Indépendance Roumaine*. So anyway, even without Claymoor on hand to record the gruesome details, it happened—the dress of young Piggy Lahovary inexplicably caught fire. She had been swathed in silk or satin which supposedly went up like a torch despite all the men's gallant attempts to put it out. The poor woman died on the way to the hospital while her clueless husband was out in Sinaia, gambling at the casino.

'How horrible,' says Sorana.

Mami Cordelia makes a little gesture with her dessert fork, as if drawing a hieroglyph, to punctuate the story's end.

But there was more. On that same fateful night, Colonel Miclescu must've realized the latent scandal of this story because he withdrew, wrote two letters—one to the military tribunal, one to his wife—and put a bullet through his head. That was in 1947, and then the communists took over, thanks in no small part to Miclescu's death.

'I'm guessing you two would still like a tour of the flat,' Mrs Jeny says to Mami Cordelia and Sorana, and I can't blame her, since she spent an entire week getting it ready, washing and ironing and stealthily cleaning the parquet floor and furniture with kerosene in preparation for just such visitors.

Flavian isn't sure if he should go along with his ladies on the tour. 'You all just stay put, we can go alone with Mrs Jeny,' says Sorana, so we stay downstairs even though we know it probably constitutes an unseemly lack of etiquette on our part.

The candles in the silver candelabra have almost burnt out, and Codrin has just passed by, tossing us a barely audible greeting on his way into the building. Aristita rushes by in her unmistakable haste, her thick tresses flowing in the breeze, and in the light of this bright summer night—as well as the yellow glow of the candles as she nears our table—it's as if she were the beauty in some famous painting, the kind of masterpiece one occasionally realizes isn't actually all that beautiful but does indeed have a certain something.

'Do you see it?'

'I'm not sure . . .'

'Just look a little closer, it's there!'

'Yes! Now I see it!'

Just a tiny spoonful of crème brulée, she says, because she's already eaten, but she loves crème brulée, 'Crème brulée is my downfall!'

Dinu and Flavian stare at her, both trying a bit too hard to look relaxed, and then the two of them clumsily go for the crème brulée at the same time. A dollop of crème falls on Dinus' T-shirt and Aristita hands him a napkin, recommending he dunk it in a bit of water first but then she immediately realizes, 'Oh, that won't help, it'll just spread it out.' She tells Dinu he can just take his shirt off and she can go wash it, since she lives right there on the ground floor. 'There's the fountain, too, in the garden,' I say, 'you can rinse it there.' 'But it's cream,' says Aristita, 'and yolks and caramelized sugar, so just water won't do.' It's as if she hasn't noticed the shirt is covered in blood and dirt, too. Or maybe she thinks it's all just crème brulée? 'I'll go get you another shirt,' says Flavian as he gets up and heads inside.

Aristita stands up, too, waiting for Dinu to hand her his shirt. He raises his arms to lift it over his head, but even before it's entirely off a flash of his freshly shaven armpits is enough for us to see the private parts of the woman tattooed all across his chest and up to his neck, one of her legs on his arm, the other down over his ribs. Aristita will certainly have glanced at the face of the tattooed woman, just as I have, and caught a glimpse of infinity, convinced that it's her face just as I'm still convinced it's mine.